MARKING TIME

TASHA CHRISTENSEN

FOR BEN

*It's easier to love every part of me when you've done
it since the beginning.*

CHAPTER ONE

WE'VE LOST MY grandmother again.

Dad and I have been here all of five minutes, and we've already misplaced the woman twice among the stacks of books, sheet music, instrument cases, and reed packets. My grandparents' above-shop apartment is so full of musical equipment I can barely see the far wall, much less the four-foot-ten woman I call "Oma."

"I'm over here!"

Her thickly accented voice seems to be coming from behind a broken sousaphone and a precarious tower of Fender amps, so I wade in that general direction. I carefully unstack the amps to reveal Oma on her hands and knees in the corner, sorting through a bin of boxed mouthpieces.

"I wanted to pull out a few options for you to try before you go to your first practice, Kendall," she says, as if that explains why a seventy-year-old woman is putting her life at risk at 9:30 in the morning. "These are some of my favorites for alto sax."

"I told you, Oma, the one I have is perfectly fine." I help her up, hands on her soft elbows. "It's gotten me this far, at least. You don't need to give me one of your nice ones. You have to sell those."

"Sure, sure, I don't *need* to." She waves me off as we emerge from the jungle of stuff into the kitchen, where my father and grandfather stand in identical positions with their hands on their hips. "But I *want* to. Let me spoil the musically inclined granddaughter I haven't seen for three years. Here."

I accept the trio of small boxes she places in my hands—three mouthpieces that cost more than we paid for my secondhand sax in the first place.

"Try these out next time you practice," Oma says. "You'll know the best one for you right away. I guarantee it."

"Thanks, Oma. Seriously."

"Now can you stop disappearing, sweetie?" Opa chides his wife. "We need to show our son and granddaughter their rooms."

Opa is tall and rail-thin, his wisp of white hair clinging to existence in a combover. Dad and I inherited his height, but we also got Oma's sturdier bones. She's a salt-of-the-earth German, raised on a farm but brilliant enough to attend Oxford, where she met my grandfather. Thick-lensed bifocals make her eyes look huge. Combined with her bulbous nose and squat frame, she comes off like an adorable cartoon caricature of a grandma.

"Yes, yes." Oma doesn't lead us down the hallway yet. Instead, she reaches up to fuss with Dad's collar in the most motherly way possible. "How was your flight? Any turbulence? Smelly seatmates?"

Dad huffs out a breath that almost sounds like laughter, and my head jerks up. I haven't heard him laugh since he learned the truth about Mom, on that horrible night last spring when everything fell apart.

He blinks as if he, too, has surprised himself.

"It was fine, Oma," I say. "Dad bought me breakfast at the airport, so I'm happy."

"Overpriced," Dad mutters, but when I glance at him, he's smiling. Being here—being *home*—is having a positive effect on him, I can already tell.

It's having an effect on me, too. My grandparents' apartment in Itaska, Minnesota, is the scene of so many memories: long childhood summers canning pears, playing speed Scrabble, and watching movies with checkered throw blankets tucked around our feet. I can't help but feel like it's finally a soft place to land. After moving nine times in twelve years, it's rare for me to step off an airplane and spend the night somewhere familiar.

I remind myself not to get too comfortable, though —this is only a temporary arrangement. And I sure wasn't expecting the huge piles of junk that have accumulated since we were last here.

"What *is* all this?" I ask Oma, gesturing at the chaos.

"Ah, yes." She purses her lips. "This. Well, we decided to clean up the shop, reorganize a bit in time for your arrival. We may have gotten a bit ambitious. It won't be here long, I promise. We just need to get these alphabetical . . . and these latches fixed up before we put them out . . ."

Then she's off, mumbling to herself as she picks up things and puts them back down.

Opa watches from the corner, smiling to himself. "Go on and get settled. Brandt, you've got your old room. Kendall, we have you on a futon in the office. We meant to get you a proper bed, but that's still in the works."

"Futons are fine. I'm not picky," I say.

I drag my suitcase and duffel bag into the office, which is less crowded than the living room. There are still a few stacks of piano learners in the corner, but I have more than enough space for the few belongings I brought with me. I've never put a lot of importance in accumulation—of things *or* people.

I sit down on the futon, which has been made up with faded floral sheets and a pillow that's gone flat over the years. Here I am. Home for the next year, until I graduate and head to Michigan for college.

I've just got to make it till then.

I unpack and get settled, content to take a break from socializing for the time being. I've been swiping through my phone for ten minutes or so when there's a knock on my door.

"Come in," I call.

Dad slides inside and leans against the wall, always moving quietly for such a big man. His thinning brown hair is rumpled, like he lay down for a rest during the short time I've been in my room. "I have a surprise for you."

My ears perk up. This is another development. Dad hasn't been the type to plan surprises lately. "What's up?"

His mouth twitches, and I can see he's barely holding in his excitement. "Follow me."

He leads me past Oma and Opa, who are bickering about the proper categorization of Beethoven sonatas, and down the stairs. At the landing, a door to the right reads "Schultz Music ~ Open 7 Days a Week ~ 10 AM–5 PM." But Dad leads me past the shop, out the back door to the muggy August heat.

"Are we making a run for it?" I ask wryly.

His mouth twitches again, but he says nothing. He plants his feet and folds his arms, looking proudly toward the parking lot. I follow his gaze.

Our bright blue rental car sits where we parked it this morning, right next to Oma and Opa's ancient station wagon, complete with wood paneling. But now, on the other side of it, is a Harley-Davidson Sportster.

I pause to check out its sleek lines and gorgeous craftsmanship. The motorcycle's seen better days, but Sportsters are no joke. I let out a whistle.

"Like it?" Dad says, and I realize what he meant when he said he had a surprise for me.

My heart leaps. "This is . . . for me?" I choke out.

Dad nods. I stare at the motorcycle, unable to believe what I'm seeing. I've never owned my own bike, though Dad taught me how to ride basically the moment I was tall enough to stay upright on one. He always kept one or two around, but he sold the ones he was fixing up before we moved here to Minnesota.

"It needs a full engine replacement," he says. "And everything else could use a good tune-up. But she's solid, and I got a great deal on her. I thought we could fix her up together."

The last few words sound scratchy, and my eyes shoot back to Dad. There's a gleam in his eyes, and I realize with shock that I feel tears coming to mine as well. I quickly swallow back the impulse and clear my throat.

"Wow," I say. "Dad. I can't believe you got this for me."

"Well, technically Opa got it," Dad says. "I found the guy on Craigslist, and Opa picked her up for me so we could surprise you. She was under a tarp when we got here, so I guess you didn't notice. If we get to work, I bet we could have her ready for you to ride to school on your first day."

My chest feels tight. "Thank you, Dad."

We don't hug, because Dad and I aren't really like that. But he reaches out and squeezes my shoulder, and all the love he needs to convey is in that gesture. Dad and I have been through a lot together in the past year. My two younger siblings, Caylee and Jackson, are back in Colorado Springs with Mom, blissfully ignorant to the details of what led to our parents' separation. They just think, as Mom puts it, that they "fell out of love."

They don't know she's a cheater.

"When does marching band start?" Dad asks me as I inspect the bike.

I sigh. I've done band for three years, but I hadn't planned to sign up at Itaska. I wanted to keep my schedule open, focus on Dad and school, but *apparently* my father and grandparents went behind my back and registered me anyway. Opa's a tuba player, Dad did euphonium, and Oma can play pretty much anything in the band *or* orchestra. Plus, my parents went to school here. I should've known they'd force me to become an Itaska Marching Raptor.

I flip through my mental checklist: Move to Minnesota. Unpack and get settled into my new life with Dad and the grandparents. Start stupid band rehearsals. "Wednesday. I should probably make sure my sax is even working."

"If it isn't, Oma can fix it up," Dad says.

Oma is the main draw behind Schultz Music, the store she runs with Opa. They sell used instruments and sheet music and other random stuff, but the reason people come from every surrounding county is because Oma's a wizard when it comes to repairs. It's like she was blessed at birth by an ancient

German fairy or something. I've watched her in the shop. When she has her hands on an out-of-tune flute or a busted trombone, nothing can stop her. She's a woman on a mission, and she *will* accomplish her goal.

"Are you nervous to start at a new school?"

I widen my eyes at Dad. He's not usually the "hover and ask questions about feelings" type.

He shakes his head. "Sorry, yeah," he says. "You don't have to answer that. How about we walk over to the hardware store and get a tool collection going? I only brought my basics from . . . from Colorado."

I don't comment on the catch in his voice, and he seems happy to lead me down the alley without any further comment. Our family had only lived in Colorado for a year before everything went down, so it's not like we have a nostalgic connection to it. In fact, I have a feeling it's the same now for Dad as it is for me: thinking about the place leaves a bad taste in my mouth.

Dad leads me down the street toward the hardware store across the river. It's early on a weekday, so the sidewalks of downtown Itaska are relatively empty. The area's old and a bit rundown, but I've always found the historic buildings and quirky shops charming. We walk past Jelly Legs Tea Shop just as the cute, elderly owner flips the sign from "Closed" to "Open." She spots us through the window and waves. I smile back. I must have met her before, when I was younger and visiting Oma and Opa. I wouldn't be surprised if half the street knows me from my childhood.

There are a few modern elements to downtown Itaska. A bike rack holds cycles that can be rented with an app on your phone. There's a store across the street that hosts tabletop gaming tournaments. And there's a girl taking a selfie on the bridge. She's dressed in tiny running shorts and a navy-blue shirt. As I watch, she tucks her phone into an armband and starts to jog in our direction. Beneath us, the Whiskey River burbles through a small set of rapids on its way out of town.

The girl looks about my age, with a slim body and muscular legs. Her twists are gathered in a high ponytail that bounces as she runs. As she draws closer, I can make out the logo on her shirt. It's a circle with two white silhouettes—the head of a hawk and the head of a dinosaur. The words "Itaska Raptors" are superimposed over the top.

So she goes to my new high school. Interesting.

As the running girl approaches, our eyes meet. Hers are brown and Disney-princess big, and despite myself, I can't seem to look away. She's *pretty*. She arches an eyebrow at me, and I realize I literally stopped in the street to stare at her.

Embarrassing.

Before my brain can work again, she passes me, her footsteps slowly drowned out by the sound of the river.

"Coming?"

I catch up to Dad, and we continue on to the hardware store.

I don't think about the running girl after that. Or at least . . . not much.

***

I SHOW UP to Itaska High School on Wednesday at 7:45 in the morning, which is way too early for summer. But that's what the director, Miss Alvarez, said in her email to me last week, so that's what I do.

My school in Colorado Springs had an entrance

with high glass windows and sleek architecture, and the lawn boasted well-trimmed hedges and careful landscaping. Itaska High is obviously older. The maroon brick exterior looks like chunks have been taken out of it, and the front courtyard is mostly composed of concrete half-walls that double as benches.

Dad pulls up to the school in our rental car and drops me off. I wave wordlessly and hitch up my backpack, which holds the sheet music Alvarez emailed me, a water bottle, and some sunscreen for practice. In my other hand is my sax, which Oma graciously tuned up last night before she went to bed (despite my not asking for it).

I have no idea where to go once inside. I'm in a big common area with a bunch of old lockers. A sign hanging from the ceiling advertises last year's yearbook. The whole place smells a little musty, like a building that hasn't been used much for the past two months, I guess. It looks like there's a lunch room past the lockers, and each corner of the large room branches off into hallways that must lead to the rest of the school.

"Need help?"

A man in a drum corps t-shirt and jeans strides toward me from the left. His long, light brown hair is pulled back in a curly ponytail, and he has a well-trimmed face of stubble.

"I'm looking for the band room." I look pointedly at his shirt. "I'm guessing you can help me?"

He chuckles. "You like the Bluecoats?"

I smirk. "More of a Phantom Regiment girl, myself."

"Ah," he says, looking suddenly grave. "Then I'm sorry to inform you that I can be of no help. I can't allow a Phantom fan into our band room."

"Understandable. Don't want anyone to realize how superior they are."

He slaps a hand to his heart. "Brutal! Are you a new student? My name's Michael Orlowski. I'm head marching tech for the band."

I shake his hand. "Kendall. Just moved here from Colorado."

"Oh, nice! Which part? I went to school in—"

I cut him off. "I only lived there a year. Don't know the area very well."

I've decided that with this move comes a new version of myself. I've never been great at picking up friends, but this year I'm making that work to my advantage. New Kendall doesn't need anyone but herself. She's doing what needs to be done, and then she's out of here.

He looks taken aback but quickly recovers. "Oh, okay. So where do you call home? Where'd you grow up?"

I think of our houses in Ohio, Illinois, Texas, and more. Not one of them felt permanent, like a place I could claim as my own.

Luckily, Michael seems to see my discomfort and pushes on. "No worries. Come on. I'll show you the way."

I follow him to the far-left corner of the locker area. We enter a plain hallway made of brick, with a few doors leading to classrooms and a boys' bathroom. He chatters harmlessly the whole way. I only reply when needed. At the end of the hallway there are two doors. The one on the left has a sign that says "Please shut quietly when performance in session." The glass door on the right opens into a lobby area with racks of chairs and instrument cases.

Michael pulls the glass door open. "After you, madam."

"Thanks."

"Welcome to the music wing of Itaska High School." Michael gestures grandly at the lobby. "We call it a wing to make ourselves feel fancy." He leads me around the exterior of the room, ticking the locations off on his fingers. "Practice rooms, offices, choir room, orchestra room. And here we are—the best place in the building."

He taps a door plaque as we enter: "BAND—ROOM 211." *Oh boy, he's one of those.*

A woman appears from around the corner, arms full of papers. She and Michael nearly collide, but he grabs her shoulders just in time to stop her momentum. His face splits into a grin.

"Gabi! We were just looking for you. I've brought you our new member."

The woman looks down at his hands on her arms and raises an eyebrow. Michael practically jumps back.

She turns her gaze to me and sticks out a hand. "You must be Kendall. I'm *Miss Alvarez*," she says with a pointed look at Michael.

"You're younger than I expected," I say as I shake her hand.

"And you're wearing a leather jacket in the summer. Everyone has their flaws."

I barely stop a snort of laughter. She's quick.

The tiniest smirk appears on her face. "Come on. Let's get you ready to march."

"I'm gonna go set up Dr. Beat," Michael says. He jogs toward an exterior door at the back of the room and calls, "See you on the field, new kid!"

I follow Miss Alvarez to the conductor's podium at the front of the room. "He's energetic."

She rolls her eyes. "You have no idea." She shuffles through a stack of papers on the podium until she pulls out a white packet, stapled at the corner. "This should have everything you need inside. Dates, show day schedules, rules, packing list. Band camp's coming up, so make sure you get all that info to a parent or guardian."

"Thanks."

"No problem." She gestures toward the back door. "I better go stop Michael before he falls off the scaffolding. Are you okay in here till practice starts?"

I nod. Then she's gone, and I'm left alone in a school I've never been to.

Not the first time that's happened.

I go to the chair she pointed out for me and set down my things. It's too early, but I put my sax together to give me something to do. It's nothing fancy, but I'm careful not to bump it on my music stand or over-twist the screw on the neck piece. Something I inherited from my Oma: a reverence for every instrument and its potential, no matter how old or scratched up it is.

Speaking of Oma, it looks like she snuck some fancy new reeds into my case along with the mouthpiece I chose from her selection. I take one from the packaging and stick it in my mouth. Ah, new reed taste. A little bitter, a little sweet, full of possibilities. Once I get my sax assembled, I try out a few scales, making my way around the circle of fourths. It takes a minute to get the reed warmed up, but eventually I'm playing a consistent sound. It sounds great. Warm, rich tone. Oma knows her stuff. I put on the mouthpiece cover to protect the reed and set the sax gently back in its case. I hear a few voices in the lobby—other students have begun to arrive—so I pull out my phone and try to look busy.

I don't follow a lot of people online. My feed is mostly relatives, band stuff, and a few Billie Eilish fan accounts. I stop at a new post from my brother, Jackson. He's posted photos of himself longboarding with friends in Garden of the Gods, this red rock park near our—*his*—house. When I lived there I would sometimes go on hikes by myself. It's a really pretty place, actually, but sometimes I'd run into kids from school and it'd be awkward. I hated making small talk with classmates. I had a few people I ate lunch with, but we didn't hang out outside of that. I didn't want to risk getting too close and then being heartbroken when we inevitably moved.

But this last time, only Dad and me moved. My siblings and Mom are still back in our split-level in Colorado Springs. Caylee and Jackson are at their schools from last year, unsure why I decided to ditch them for Minnesota. I miss them badly, but I couldn't stay with Mom, not after finding out she'd been cheating on Dad for two years.

I was the one who discovered her indiscretion. I'd borrowed her phone to use the camera, and a message from a guy whose name I didn't recognize popped up. He didn't say anything explicit, just "Last night was amazing. Let's do it again soon." But Mom had said she was at a work dinner the night before, and it hit me as strange. So I talked to Dad, and he was the one who figured it all out and got Mom to confess. I had to referee as their marriage fell apart in a single day.

Dad's always struggled with depression, but finding out about Mom broke him. He always looks like he's on the verge of tears, and there have been a lot of times when he's staring off into space and I have to say his name multiple times to get his attention. There are bags under his eyes that make it clear he's not sleeping much, and he barely puts effort into making or eating food.

Things have been up and down since we got to Oma's and Opa's. Opa loves to cook and Dad's too polite to turn it down, so at least he's been getting three square meals. We've also spent a lot of time working on my new bike, and I can tell that cheers him up. But in the evening, he disappears to his room while I work through old game show episodes with my grandparents. He sleeps late, and those eye bags don't seem to be going anywhere. I can only hope starting his new job at the auto shop across town will build on his progress.

I'm startled out of my broody thoughts by the sound of a scream from the hallway. I jump up, phone forgotten in my hand, and race to the doorway. I'm emerging when the scream trails off into hysterical laughter.

My heart's still pounding as two girls push into the lobby, giggling. Following them is a tall guy in a snapback hat. When they see me, they all stop and look up.

"Are . . . you okay?" one of the girls says, and it's then that I realize she's the Disney princess I saw jogging the other day by the river. I also realize I'm breathing hard and my jaw is dangling, because I was pretty certain I was about to stumble upon a murder scene. I snap my mouth shut.

Recognition dawns on the girl's face. Now that she's not sweaty and wearing workout clothes, I can tell she's not just pretty—she's stunning. Her skin is deep brown and flawless, her big eyes framed by long eyelashes, her hair in immaculate box twists.

She smiles, revealing straight, white teeth. "Hey, I know you! Carina, remember I told you about that girl who stared at me while I was running?"

Carina is basically Wednesday Addams in yoga pants. Unlike her friend, this girl's so pale her skin has a blue undertone. She looks me up and down. "Yeah. This her?"

My entire body shouts at me to run away and never step foot on school grounds again. My insides have melted from sheer embarrassment, and my tongue feels like a cactus in my mouth. I couldn't speak if I tried.

"I didn't know you went to our school," Disney Princess says. Her tone is hard to read. "Hey, why were you staring at me?"

I force my mouth to work. "Uh, I wasn't staring at you."

"No?"

I nod once, then twice for good measure. "I saw your shirt. Was trying to figure out why it had two mascots."

"Uh-huh." She doesn't sound convinced, but the curl of her mouth tells me she's decided to cut me some slack. "Well, you're in luck, 'cause I was a freshman when it went down. We're the Itaska Raptors. The mascot's supposed to be a hawk, but for years everyone insisted it was a velociraptor. Even crowdfunded a suit. Eventually administration got fed up and said we could have both."

"That's . . ." *Actually hilarious.* ". . . Strange."

The girl's eyes dance with something I can't make out. Curiosity? Flirting? *Stop overthinking it.*

"I'm Jaz Whitaker," she says to me, then gestures

to the others. "Carina is my best friend, and Emilio is probably my fourth or fifth favorite friend." Emilio punches her arm, and she grins. "We play percussion."

"My name's Kendall." I shrug, though there's nothing to shrug about. "Alto sax."

"Ah, my brother will be glad to hear that," Jaz says without elaborating further. "Anyway, we're gonna go get ready in the Cave. See you out there?"

I had no idea this school had a cave, but I let it slide before I embarrass myself further. "See ya."

She and her friends disappear into the band room, and I'm left stunned, standing in the afterglow of Jaz Whitaker.

CHAPTER TWO

PRACTICE STARTS OUT on the field. I leave my riding jacket on my chair and shuffle outside with everyone else, trying to call as little attention to myself as possible. As long as I avoid making a splash on the first day, I figure I'll fly under the radar for the rest of my time in Itaska. New Kendall isn't here to make friends.

I follow the group past a dumpster and down a hill, cutting through a football practice field with trim turf and bright white lines. On the far side, the band's own field has been carved out of overgrown grass and a perimeter of maples and oaks. A rickety scaffold towers over a single drum major podium. *Yikes. Not much to look at.*

So far Minnesota's weather reminds me of my time living in Illinois, where the worst part of summer wasn't the heat but the bugs and humidity. Speaking of heat—I've forgotten to bring sunscreen. I hope the outside part of practice is short, because there's no way I'm approaching anyone to borrow some.

The head drum major, a guy with flaming red hair, calls the band to the podium. Michael and Miss Alvarez sit on the edge. His legs are swinging, while she has an elbow coolly propped on her knee. It's the first official day of marching band practice, though the band's met a couple times throughout the summer, so Miss Alvarez gives a little welcome spiel. Her comments are quick and to-the-point—my kind of teacher.

Michael pipes in after she finishes. "And welcome to all the freshmen and new members!" He gestures for everyone to clap. "You're going to have a great time in Itaska Band, and we're so glad to have you. This is a life-changing experience, and I encourage you all to be outgoing and take advantage of this opportunity to make friends and build your community before the first day of school. In fact, why don't we each turn and introduce ourselves to someone right now. Find a person you don't recognize and say hi."

I freeze like I'm surrounded by T-Rexes. If I don't move, they can't see me, right? People mill around, slapping high fives and making awkward small talk. I think for a moment that I may have lucked out until I feel a tap on my shoulder. I turn around to find a Black boy a foot shorter than me with a silver-plated alto saxophone in his hands. He's skinny and young, with cropped hair and cubic zirconium studs in his ears.

"Hey, fellow sax!" he says with a voice that definitely hasn't dropped yet. "I'm Adam, and I'm a freshman. Who are you?"

"Kendall," I say. "Senior."

"So what should I know about being in the band? Got any upper-classman wisdom to impart?"

I rub the back of my neck, wishing we could just get to the *practice* part of band practice. "I'm actually new, too. So I'm about as useless to you as you are to me."

I realize as the words are coming out that they're a lot harsher than I intended. But Adam only shrugs and laughs.

"Well, maybe we can figure stuff out together," he says. "I could use a friend. All I've got is my sister over there, and she told me not to embarrass her."

He points across the band. I stand on tip-toes to see the person he's speaking about, and my stomach flips.

"Jaz is your sister?" It's just my luck that her brother's decided I'm his new best friend. I guess she did warn me.

Jaz is chatting with the guy she entered the band lobby with. They're both in marching harnesses—Jaz wears a snare, and he has a set of quad drums. Apparently *they* don't have to introduce themselves to someone new.

"Sure is." Adam jumps up and waves. "Jasmine! Hey! Over here!"

Jaz rolls her eyes but smiles wryly and returns his wave. Then her gaze moves to me, and it lights up with that curiosity again. I can't help it; I look away. I don't like all this attention both the Whitakers have decided to give me. I don't have the patience for a family full of extroverts.

I'm relieved when Miss Alvarez calls the band back to order. "All right, that's enough chit-chat. We've got a lot to learn, and our first show is in twenty-three days. You all should've brought a small notebook to mark your dots, correct? Let's see 'em."

Great. Another thing I'm unprepared for. There was a flurry of emails when Dad signed me up for band, but with the move, a lot apparently slipped through the cracks. A new wave of irritation rises up that I'm even here in the first place.

"Perfect," she says. "And who forgot? Raise your hands, people. Public shaming is an essential part of the Itaska Band experience."

A couple hands go up, mostly freshman. I bite my lip. I know I have to fess up, but I feel like an idiot. Sunscreen is one thing, but I've been in band for years. I should know better than to forget a dot book.

Right before I lift my arm, Michael pipes up. "No worries, people. If you need a notebook, I have a few extra in my bag. Come by after basics and I'll set you up."

I immediately drop my half-raised arm, relief coursing through me. Jeez, we haven't even started rehearsal and I'm already exhausted.

The rest of the morning is significantly less stressful. Michael directs us through some marching basics, patiently correcting the freshmen when they fail to snap up their instruments on time after the fifth try. After basics, we receive a stack of tiny sheets that outline exactly where we should be on the field during each bar of music in our show. I discreetly pick up an extra notebook from Michael, and the band spends some time in the shade gluing in the papers, page by page. Adam spends the whole time talking about how cool Jaz is, and I spend the whole time trying not to fixate on her.

Next, Alvarez gathers us back into the band room for instrument warm-ups. "Our show this year is called 'Flight,' and it's centered around the journey of the Wright Brothers. So we're really going to work on cultivating a tone and blend that soars."

She walks us through an exercise to open our throats and palates. I try not to think about how stupid I must look. Then we're finally playing our instruments, working through a packet of scales and intonation exercises. We've just barely started on the first page of show music when the clock reaches noon and we're all dismissed for lunch.

I didn't bring anything to eat, and Dad dropped me off, so my food options are limited. My phone tells me there's a convenience store with a deli just down the street from the school, and that's about it. Good enough for me. Neither of my parents is great in the kitchen, so I've learned to be happy with sandwiches and frozen pizzas and cereal. I pack up my stuff and start the walk.

I'm hardly twenty feet down the road when I hear, "Hey! New girl!"

My shoulders tense up. I turn to see Jaz hanging out the passenger side of a beater sedan, grinning from ear to ear. Carina's in the driver's seat, looking like she'd rather invite a live bear into her car. Or is that just her normal face? Hard to tell.

I can barely see Adam in the back through the tinted windows. Jaz wallops the side of the car.

"Come to lunch with us," she says as they pull up alongside me. "We're hitting up Pak's."

The car sputters and chokes before it returns to idling. The thing looks like it's getting by on vibes alone.

"I'm good," I say. "I'm walking to the deli. In the mood for a sad veggie sandwich."

Jaz laughs. "Come on! Pak's is tradition. It's a Chinese-slash-Italian buffet across the river. It'll change your life."

"Honestly, that sounds horrific."

She whacks the side of the car again. She's obviously used to people going along with her plans. "Not taking no for an answer, new girl! Get in the car or I'll sic Adam on you."

Adam grins mischievously through the dark window. I don't wait to find out what "siccing" him would entail.

"Fine," I grumble, getting into the other side of the car. It smells like flavored vapes and body spray.

"All right, let's do this!" Jaz whoops. "I'm starving!"

Carina and Jaz sing along to Doja Cat as we cruise down the road, going at least fifteen over the speed limit. Adam nods to the music, fidgeting with a small puzzle toy in his hands.

After a few minutes, he turns to me. "You don't talk much, do you?"

"Not if I can help it."

The music continues. The front-seaters are nearly shouting the lyrics.

"That's cool," he says. "I like quiet people. They pay attention to stuff."

"Hm."

"You're really determined not to be my friend, aren't you?" He doesn't sound hurt, just like he's making an observation.

"That's not it, exactly."

"But it kind of is." Now there *is* a little bit of hurt in his voice.

I sigh, long and slow, and finally turn to face him. "Okay, you win. We can be friends, little freshman. But you've got to realize I'm not into talking much. It's just . . . not my thing."

"Fine with me." Before I can feel relieved, he says, "I'm happy to do all the talking around here!"

And that's how I end up in the back of a car learning more about the newest *Star Wars* cartoon than I ever cared to know.

Not a moment too soon, we pull into a strip mall parking lot. Between a cute boba shop and a run-down tailor, a gaudy sign declares "Pak's Italian & Chinese ALL YOU CAN EAT Buffet." One of those ceramic lucky cat figurines, bedecked in a huge, curly mustache and a chef's hat, waves from the window. Props for committing to the bit, I guess.

Jaz leads the way inside and to the front podium. "Table for . . ." she trails off, looking to Carina. "How many, do you think?"

Four? I almost offer, but then three more cars pull into the parking lot and vaguely familiar people start pouring out. There's the red-headed drum major, the rest of the saxophone section, and a few color guard in cropped tank tops and leggings. A girl with gorgeous curly hair is getting helped into a wheelchair by a big dude in a tie-dye shirt.

There are so many people outside—at least a dozen. Every muscle in my body tightens up. I do *not* do big gatherings, especially when I don't know anyone. But then Jaz bumps my arm and gestures for me to follow her, and I can't think of any excuse or way to escape. This is my punishment for not going all-in on New Kendall. Next time a pretty girl invites me into her car, I'm sprinting away like a kid who just learned about stranger danger.

Our server greets Jaz by name and doesn't seem alarmed at the sudden crowd. He takes our drink orders while we wait for everyone to come in. I almost order chocolate milk before stopping myself. Before everything, Mom and Dad used to take us to whatever buffet was in our current town at least once a month. We'd always order chocolate milk, no matter how old we got.

I order iced tea instead. A Chinese-Italian place probably doesn't even have chocolate milk.

Jaz takes it upon herself to introduce everyone as they arrive at the table. The dimpled quad player, whose name I had definitely forgotten until this point, is Emilio. The drum major is Gavin. The curly-haired girl is Alyssa Valentine, and she is apparently inseparable from Matty Labiche, the guy who helped her in the parking lot.

"They're not dating, but they should be," Jaz whispers as Matty pulls out a chair for Alyssa. "Don't tell them I said that, though. We're letting them get to it in their own time."

I nod sagely as if I understand what's going on. Adam picks up the baton to introduce me to the other two people in the sax section. Jake Novak, the tenor player, is a quiet, sullen junior with hair that covers his eyes. Madison Diquattro plays bari sax, which is impressive, since she looks about five feet tall. Must be packing some muscles under that bright pink baseball tee. Adam informs me Madison's the section leader, as well.

"And not just because she's dating the drum major," Jaz adds in a fake whisper.

Color guard intros come last. I wave and say hi, absolutely positive I will forget everyone in less than five minutes. Everyone seems nice—too nice. It's overwhelming. Add in the fact that the volume in the restaurant has risen twenty decibels, and I'm starting to look for escape routes.

Jaz must sense my discomfort, because she nudges my arm again and stands up. "Shall we?"

I try to ignore the fact that my skin tingles where she touched me. "Lead the way."

Jaz and I wind through the buffet tables, filling

our plates with an eclectic mix of stir fry, pasta, and deep-fried foods. We don't speak, but I find myself constantly aware of where she is in relation to me. It's like my body is developing a sensor that's attuned to her position in space at all times, and it bothers me. I don't want to notice that Jaz chooses brown rice instead of white, or that she keeps all the food on her plate carefully separated. Yet here I am, gathering up these little details about her like a greedy squirrel preparing for winter.

"I wouldn't get that if I were you."

I'm about to pick up some kind of vegetarian stromboli with a set of tongs. "Why not?"

Jaz shrugs. "Madison got the meat one once, and it made her sick. We steer clear now."

"Yeah, but this one's vegetarian." I hold it up, inspecting the contents. "It's got, like, sun-dried tomatoes. They probably used bad salami or something."

"It was pepperoni."

I wave that away. "I have a strong stomach. It'll be fine."

"Suit yourself." She arches a perfect eyebrow. "Those things have bad energy. That's all I'm saying."

Back at the table, Jaz announces that I am braving the Cursed Stromboli, which causes half the table to erupt into spontaneous applause. I hear someone murmur, "So brave," like I'm about to sacrifice myself in a war. Jaz shoots me a wink before digging into her own food, and my stomach does a somersault.

How am I supposed to eat now? I feel my cheeks warm. Jaz eats placidly, as if she didn't just wink at me in a possibly flirty way. I must be misinterpreting. What are the chances someone like her is into girls? It must have been a friendly wink. Or a "good luck with your stromboli" wink.

I shake my head and dive into my food, studiously avoiding eye contact with Jaz for the rest of the meal. She tries to talk to me a few times, but I keep my responses monosyllabic, and eventually she gives up. I'm thrown off by her—she's just so *much*. She's outgoing, she's pretty, and she pays attention to me in a way that makes my body feel too big for my skin.

This is . . . not good. I've had a few crushes over the years, but they can never really turn into anything. I've kissed exactly one person, a girl in Illinois who was probably the closest to a boyfriend or girlfriend that I've ever had. We'd sneak out during P.E. sometimes, but that was it. My family moved to California in the middle of that school year.

I thought I'd gotten a handle on the crush thing. I left that behind with Old Kendall.

I decide to focus on conversations with the rest of the table, the lesser of two evils. Turns out I don't have to talk much. Bari Sax Madison regales the group with wild stories about past band trips. Everyone laughs at the good memories, even Adam, who has apparently heard these all from his sister. Matty crafts a strangely beautiful rendering of *The Starry Night* from spaghetti that has everyone getting up to take photos. I have about five followers on Instagram—probably because I post, like, once a year—so I keep my phone in my pocket.

Afterwards, I climb again into the backseat of Carina's car. Adam offers me a dinner mint from the handful he grabbed at the restaurant. I decline politely.

I poke at my arms, which are decidedly more red than they were this morning. Me and my stupid sunscreen pride. Jaz has apparently picked up on my cold shoulder, because she doesn't try to talk to me on the way back. Adam has come full circle back to talking about *Star Wars,* so I stare out the window and occasionally respond as needed. We're in a typical suburban area, with a gas station and a pharmacy and a run-down Burger King on the corner. We drive past a theater with a full marquee, and conversation turns to the latest *Fast & Furious* movie. If I wanted to make friends, I'd chime in about how *Fast & Furious* is mine and Dad's favorite series to watch together. I even met Vin Diesel in person at Chicago Comic Con.

But I don't want to make friends, so I say nothing. Besides, I'm starting to feel a little queasy.

***

HALF AN HOUR into afternoon practice, my face literally *feels* green. I didn't know that was possible. I can't make a sound on my saxophone, because every time I tense my abs to blow out air, I feel like it might not just be air that'll come out.

Adam looks me up and down. "You okay, Kendall? You're sweating."

I nod, not trusting myself to speak. Miss Alvarez calls out a rehearsal number, and I flip my page to the appropriate spot.

Out of the corner of my eye, I see Adam pull out his phone and type something. Then he puts it on the stand and continues playing with the rest of the band. I mime through the notes, willing myself not to lose my lunch. When I sneak a glance back at percussion (sue me), Jaz has her phone out, thumbs flying. Adam's screen lights up.

Is he snitching on me? Telling Jaz I feel sick? I don't get why these two siblings are suddenly so concerned about me, a complete stranger they literally met today. A wave of irritation washes over me.

Followed closely by a wave of nausea. I need to go —now.

There's no time to raise my hand and ask to go to the bathroom. I unclip my sax, plunk it on my chair —breaking the reed in the process—and stumble to the exit.

I hear Miss Alvarez say, "Uh, okay," but there's no way I'm stopping now. I burst into the hallway. I find a boys' bathroom, but for some stupid reason the girls' isn't right next to it. I wander, desperate, until I hear my name.

"Kendall!" It's Jaz, because of course it is. "Over here."

She motions toward a door in a completely different hallway, which makes no sense, but I don't have time to worry about the logic of this school's blueprints. I sprint toward her, slide into the bathroom, and barely make it to a stall before I heave into the toilet bowl.

It. Is. Nasty. I throw up a few more times, and by the end I'm more barfing because of how gross it is than anything else. I feel dramatic and miserable and sorry for myself. *This is the worst. I'm done with life. Please, anything for this nightmare to end.*

And then it does end, and I'm sitting on the floor, emptied out. My throat burns.

"You good?"

Jaz stands over me, brow wrinkled with concern. Great. I grab some toilet paper and angrily wipe my mouth. Why did she have to stick around? My embarrassment is through the roof and halfway to outer space.

"Obviously not," I croak.

I wait for her to say "I told you so," to mock me for eating the stromboli, but it doesn't come. Her eyes stay concerned.

"Were you standing there for all that?" I ask her.

"No." *Oh, thank god.* "I was outside the door. Figured you didn't want company while you prayed to the porcelain god. But now that you're done, let's get you some water."

I begrudgingly accept her arm, and she helps me to the sink. I rinse my mouth out and sip straight from the faucet, then dry my face off with the paper towels. When I'm done, she's there with a mint like the one Adam offered me in the car.

"Thanks." I accept it. "I'm okay to go back now, I think."

"We're not going anywhere." She leans toward me and stage whispers, "You look *terrible.*"

"Wow, thanks."

She giggles, and despite everything, my insides light up knowing I caused such an adorable noise. We sit on the floor outside the bathroom, backs against the maroon brick wall.

"Sorry you had to hear all that."

"Not a big deal, seriously. Half the time I'll puke before a performance or a track meet. I am well acquainted with the sights and sounds."

"Gross."

She shrugs, grinning. "That's life, baby. Sometimes you just gotta hurl."

"You get nervous, then? You don't seem like the type." *Stop asking her about herself, Kendall.*

"Oh yeah, *stupid* nervous. No matter how good I am or how much I've practiced. When the time rolls around, my brain and body just straight up lose it."

"And then you win it."

"Usually." She narrows her eyes. "How'd you know that?"

"Adam can't shut up about you. Told me you're battery captain, track captain, pretty much captain of everything. Maybe a pirate, too? Honestly wouldn't be surprised."

Annnd she's giggling again. I need to stop doing that.

"I think I feel better now." I shoot to my feet and start heading for the band room.

"Are you sure?"

I'm already ten feet ahead of her. "Yep. Let's go."

"Okay . . ." I hear her get up and follow me. "Kendall, did I do something wrong?"

I don't slow down. "Nope. We've just missed too much practice. I've got a lot to catch up on still."

"All right," she agrees softly. She doesn't say anything else.

I don't look Jaz's way the rest of the day. Adam keeps bugging me about how I'm feeling, but I assure him I'm good. I throw on a new reed from Oma's box to replace the one I broke. And when practice is over, I leave before anyone can stop me.

***

THAT SATURDAY MY body wakes me up way too early and won't let me fall back asleep. I lie on my futon mattress, finding patterns in the popcorn ceiling, until a ray of sunlight between the curtains starts to blind me. I get up and get dressed. Dad and I are going to work on the bike today, so I throw on a raggedy pair of sweats and a black T-shirt with a Dayton High School logo on it. The shirt's covered in gray splatters from the time we renovated a fixer-upper in Texas. The memory of combing dried paint out of Caylee's stick-straight hair sends a pang through my heart. My little sister has always been the quietest, sweetest kid in the entire world. Dad and I have done regular video calls with her and Jackson since we've been here, but my siblings and I have never been apart for this long. Being separated like this is a lot harder than I thought it would be.

I shoot off a text to the two of them.

Kendall 6:59 am
Miss your faces!

Caylee 7:08 am
Miss yours more!

Jackson 7:10 am
You just saw my face yesterday. Get a grip

I didn't expect replies right away, since it's an hour earlier in Colorado. Then I remember Caylee mentioned a big dance competition this weekend. Mom must have dragged Jackson out of bed to come with, which explains his grumpy reply. Not that fully rested Jackson would have been much more chipper.

Kendall 7:11 am
Good luck today, Caylee!

In the kitchen, Opa and Dad are quietly drinking coffee and eating muesli with raisins on top. I pour myself a bowl and dig around until I find some bananas and raspberries. Fresh fruit on muesli > dried fruit on muesli. I drink water, since I'm not into coffee. In fact, I don't really like any non-water drinks. It's always weirded out Jackson, a Baja Blast addict, and Mom, who usually has a cup of Coke Zero or a glass of wine in hand.

I ignore the tightness in my chest and wolf down breakfast in between the two silent, stalwart Mathis men. That is, until we hear a bellow from below that sounds like a hippopotamus riding into battle.

The three of us look at each other. Dad's mouth is full of muesli, and a trickle of milk drips down his chin. Everyone's expressions say, "Please don't make me investigate."

I've somehow managed to finish before both of them—they eat slower than a 50cc scooter—so I venture downstairs to explore the source of the noise. The shop isn't open yet, and it's dark enough inside that I have to walk with my hands outstretched to avoid knocking over the rack of guitars or shelves filled with *Standard of Excellence* books. The only light comes from the back corner of the shop, where a single bulb hangs over Oma's workbench. She's kneeling on her stool, elbows flapping as she cranks the tuning knobs of a child-sized cello. One of the strings is disconnected and has curled up, and it keeps poking her in the face. German curse words flow freely from her mouth.

"Everything okay down here, Oma?"

Her head swivels up with a deep frown. She's got a little magnifying headset on that makes her look like a crazed inventor. Her hair, silver tinged with brown, has been wrestled into a haphazard ponytail, but so many wisps have gotten out that I can hardly tell there's an elastic in there.

"Eh?' Her eyes move toward me, then she pushes up the headset. "Oh, it's you, Kendall. Thought you were a customer. Do you need something?"

"I heard you yell," I say. "Are you all right?"

"Yes, yes," she replies in a tone of voice that says everything is, in fact, not all right. "Just having some trouble with this *sch*—with this darn cello." Oma tries not to swear in German around me, even though I only know what a few of them mean. "The tuning pegs keep slipping. I'd usually use Opa for an extra set of hands, but his eyes are going. Don't know if you know he has cataracts."

"I did not," I say.

"Here." She reaches out and drags me toward the bench. "You help me."

"I'm supposed to go work on the bike with Dad . . ." I protest weakly.

"Don't worry. It'll only take a minute."

She shows me where to hold the cello and when to apply pressure, and I hold still as she replaces the pegs and re-attaches the strings in a way that makes them less likely to slip. Now that she has my help, she's in her element: quick and methodical, like this is a dance she memorized long ago. She works on instruments the way Dad works on cars.

As if on cue, Dad's voice emerges from the far end of the shop. "Everybody alive in here?" he calls.

"Everything is fine, good, yes," Oma snaps. "Honestly, you Mathises are always so cautious. Kendall's just helping me for a minute. We're done now. Go fix your overpriced bicycle."

"Love you, Mama," Dad says.

"Love you, my *Bärli*."

Dad's entire face crinkles up when he smiles, all the way from his dimpled chin to his green eyes to his receding hairline. I look exactly like him in pictures, minus the hairline. The genuine happiness on his face makes my throat tighten. I haven't seen that expression much since he and Mom broke up. Being here with his parents, in the home he grew up in, has been doing my dad good. He had me scared for a while there, in the darkest parts of his depression.

I follow Dad out back. He lays out the tools and equipment he brought, then gets to work showing me what we need to fix. He's a lot more patient than Oma as he demonstrates everything and reminds me about safety. Finally, he lets me get up in the bike's guts and start working.

After a period of quiet, Dad says, "So how's marching band?"

I shoot him a look. *Are we doing the small talk thing now?* He shrugs innocently.

I roll my eyes. "It's fine. I like the music well enough. You forgot to pay for band camp, by the way. I need to get a check and a signature from you by Monday."

"Sorry. I can do that."

We work in silence again for a while, then for some reason, he decides to interrogate me further. "Have you made any friends yet? At band?"

"Da-a-a-d," I draw it out as long as I can, ending on a gurgling sound like I'm dying.

But he's serious. We're doing the small talk thing.

"I don't need to make friends, Dad," I say. "I just have to survive senior year and get out of there. If I make all these friends, then I'll be sad when I leave them. It's way easier to just . . . not."

I glance at Dad. He's watching me with this sad

expression, his eyebrows drawn together and his mouth turned down. I don't like making him sad—he gets enough of that as it is.

"What?" I huff.

"I hate to hear you talking like that, Kendall," he says. "I hate that your mom's job and all this moving and divorce drama has taken your teen years and turned them into something that has to be survived. I had such a good time in high school with my friends."

"You did?" Dad doesn't reminisce about high school much. I figured he was like me, basically a ghost who walked the halls and got by without making trouble. Or relationships. Same thing, really.

"Antonio, Randy, and Valerie," he says, staring at a speck on the sidewalk. "They were my peeps." I make a face at his old-man slang, but he continues unbothered. "We did everything together. Wind ensemble, marching band, quartets. Antonio and I signed up for our first metal shop classes together— he was the reason I became a mechanic. Valerie and Randy started dating junior year, but we all stayed friends."

He practically has stars in his eyes now. It's like he's forgotten I'm there. "I remember so many nights of sneaking out to go to the twenty-four-hour diner down the street. We'd argue about *Batman* or whatever while the waitress brought us soda refills, until they got sick of us loitering. I remember going with the band to California, playing at a competition in the Rose Bowl Stadium. Wow, was that something special."

He blinks, finally seeming to register that he's here with his daughter, who's lying under a broken-down motorcycle behind his parents' house. For a moment there, he was somewhere else entirely.

"Anyway," he says. "High school can be a great experience. I haven't talked to any of those guys in years. We lost touch after everyone got married and started having babies. But I have no regrets about those nights in the diner or the hours laughing in shop class. Those memories last forever."

I stare at him. "I think that's the most words I've ever heard come out of your mouth."

He reddens. "Don't be silly." He pauses, eyes narrowed in thought. "But think about what I said, Kendall. This is a special time in your life. Don't let your mom and me screw it up."

CHAPTER THREE

AH, THE FIRST morning of band camp. The sun is shining, and the world is full of possibilities. Our spirits have not yet been broken by a week of twelve-hour practice days.

Everyone buzzes with excitement as we climb onto the buses that will take us up north. Band parents stack suitcases and instruments into the band trailer. Michael, the ponytailed marching tech, and Gavin, the drum major, stand at their respective buses to give out high fives as people enter. Miss Alvarez supervises the chaos with a clipboard.

"Gimme some skin, Kendall Mathis!" Michael has memorized everyone's first and last names, apparently, and is showing that off as we get onto the bus. I fist bump his open palm, and he cackles. "Love it. Everything going well after your first few days?"

I glance back at the line piling up behind me. "Yeah. It's fine," I say and hurry onto the bus to cut off any more conversation. I'm not a big fan of Michael—he's too nice. I prefer Miss Alvarez, who doesn't seem to care much whether I live or die.

Speaking of people who are too nice: Jaz waves at me from the second-to-last row of the bus. The seat next to her is open. Despite the barfing, she's kept up her attempts to make me feel included since my first day with the band last week. Honestly, I wouldn't be surprised to find out Michael put her up to all this. There's no way someone's this welcoming on their own.

I've mostly managed to hold Jaz off, although I *have* let Adam a little bit into my bubble. Mostly because I can't get away from the only other person who plays alto sax. He, however, has ended up on the second bus with a few freshmen he's started to bond with. So here I am, alone and trying to decide who to sit with.

I wave back to Jaz and very deliberately take the open seat next to the guy in front of her. He's the percussionist with dimples I have been introduced to multiple times, whose name I *still* cannot remember. Luckily, we seem to wordlessly establish a mutual understanding to leave each other alone. I stick in my AirPods and he turns around to talk to Jaz and Carina, who took the other spot after shooting me what I could only interpret as a death glare. What is that girl's deal? Do she and Jaz have a thing? They haven't been touchy with each other, not that I've been paying attention. I usually assume girls are straight until proven otherwise. Jaz has sure been giving me *vibes,* but . . . I don't know. I'm probably just being stupid.

The trip gets going, and I watch the countryside pass by to the tunes of Billie Eilish. I get almost a full hour of peace, watching the suburbs turn to farms and trees and lakes. I have a faint memory of a camping trip with Opa in Minnesota once. A bear ate all our food on the first night, despite our stringing it up between two trees to keep it out of reach. I wonder if we're headed to a similar area. Geography has never been my strong suit.

My peace is disturbed when my seatmate taps me on the shoulder. So much for a mutual understanding.

I take out my earbuds. "What?"

"We're arguing about whether there are real UFO sightings," he explains, as if that's an entirely normal conversation to force me into. "Me, Alyssa, and Jaz say yes. Carina, Matty, and Madison say no. We need a tie-breaker."

I sigh, realizing that I will not be allowed to return to my blissful solitude. "Well, it seems to me if there were intelligent life out there, they'd be smart enough to realize we're a hot mess here on Earth. Nothing worth making contact with."

"That's what I said!" Madison crows. She's halfway through French braiding her platinum blond hair, but she pauses to give me a high five across the aisle.

Jaz shifts so she's on her knees, hands braced against the back of our seat. "No, no, even if that were true, they would *still* have to send out some kind of probes to figure out that we *are* a hot mess they shouldn't make contact with . . . and those would be *unidentified flying objects.*"

I snort. "They don't even need to come here to realize how stupid humanity is. They just need to catch some signals from afar. Have you *listened* to AM radio?" I almost say *I* have, because my mom's dad was super into it, but I hold back. Even if I've been roped into this conversation, I don't have to reveal things about my life and family.

"You guys are just so painfully wrong," Jaz shoots back, obviously enjoying herself. "There are literal declassified government videos showing UFOs. I'm serious—look it up!"

I just shrug. "Sorry. I'm in the anti-UFO camp."

Carina, Madison, and Matty cheer.

The conversation quickly moves on to a new topic, but Jaz shoots out a hand toward me. "Gimme your phone."

"What? Why?"

"I will *send* you those videos. Prove you're wrong." She pats the seat impatiently, just like she did while trying to convince me to go to the dreaded Italian-Chinese buffet. "Just give me the phone, Mathis."

"Oh, so we're on last name terms?" I begrudgingly hand over my iPhone.

Jaz opens my messenger app, types in a phone number, and sends a text to herself. Then she pulls out her own phone, pastes a link, and hits send. I pull out the adorable baggie of snacks Opa packed for me, trying to keep myself busy. A package of honey mustard pretzel bites, a Ziploc of apple slices with lemon juice, and my favorite—Reese's Pieces. I know what I'm eating first.

Jaz hands me my phone. I snatch it back, feeling violated. The grainy U.S. Navy videos of strange floating objects *are* rather convincing, but I'm not about to tell Jaz that. "Hm. Pretty interesting. I guess we can agree to disagree."

"Agree to disagree is a coward's move," Jaz crows. "You know I'm right!"

"Kendall! Jaz!" Madison butts in. "We're playing Truth or Dare, ladies. You have no choice in the matter."

"Who are you people, my parents?" I mutter.

"Nope!" Madison says. "But we *are* your fellow band members, and you're new. Consider this your initiation, and be grateful you got off easily. Last year we made Hayden Polski eat a grasshopper."

I almost choke on my Reese's Pieces.

"Is that a yes?"

"*No.*"

Madison looks taken aback. "Fine. Be that way." She turns to the rest of the group. "I'll start. Matty, truth or dare?"

Matty gulps. "Dare."

Madison taps her fingers together like she's an evil genius. "Switch shirts with Jaz."

She cackles maniacally while Jaz and Matty groan.

"No fair!" Jaz complains. "It's not my dare!"

"Don't act all modest, Jaz. You love taking your shirt off," Carina chips in.

I narrowly avoid death by choking for a second time. I scramble for my water bottle and chug some down.

Jaz scrunches up her nose. "Fine. Matty, you ready to do this?"

Matty nods solemnly. "I'm glad it's you, honestly. You wear nice, stretchy athletic shirts."

He reaches up over his head and pulls at his collar. He's a big dude, and it turns out there's definitely some muscle going on underneath that Grateful Dead tee. My guy crushes are usually leaner, but I can see the appeal. A few of the girls whistle as he hams it up, flexing like a bodybuilder. I chuckle. Then Jaz tugs off her shirt to reveal a hot pink sports bra, and my laugh turns into a strangled sound.

Our eyes meet for just a second, and I swear she smirks.

I dart my gaze away, clearing my throat. *Stare at the floor. Out the window. Anywhere else.* I don't look back until everyone is safely shirted again.

When I hazard a glance at Jaz, I'm relieved to see she now looks ridiculous. Matty's tie-dye T-shirt is huge on her.

But a little part of me worries that *Jaz* is the one who's seen too much. Does she know I'm into girls now? Does she know I'm into *her*?

"My turn," Matty says, looking twice as ridiculous in Jaz's tiny shirt. "Carina, truth or dare?"

"I'm lazy," she says. "Truth." Everyone boos, but she's unruffled. "I'm not about to take off my shirt."

"Okay." Matty takes longer than Madison to think —I suspect she has a whole arsenal of Truth or Dare ideas built up in her head for just this situation. "Have you ever cheated on someone?"

My mind immediately goes to Mom, to her texts, to the look in Dad's eyes when he learned the truth about his marriage. She's never even said sorry for tearing our family apart with her selfishness.

I don't want to think about that this week. Despite being basically forced to go, I do like band camp. It's this weird time when I feel like the rest of the world doesn't exist. No matter where I've gone to school, band camp has been a time to shut out the noise and just focus on show music and aching muscles and dots on a field. If I'm here, I'm going to make it count.

"Never cheated," Carina says to the question. "I'm a one-guy type of girl."

So she *is* straight. I'm embarrassed by how relieved that makes me.

The game continues for the rest of the bus ride. Someone ends up doing a freestyle rap about tubas. A few embarrassing stories are told. At one point, my seatmate—Emilio, I've finally remembered—has to go to the front of the bus, sit next to Miss Alvarez, and ask her obnoxious questions about her relationship (or lack thereof) with Michael. She says something that apparently wrecks Emilio, because he comes back with his tail between his legs.

"That was terrible." He shudders, not elaborating further. "Okay, Jaz, truth or dare."

"You know what the answer is." She grins.

"Go to Emma Bissett's Instagram page." Jaz starts to protest, but he continues on. "Scroll down to something at least a year old and like it."

Jaz covers her face with her hands, obviously mortified. My stomach doesn't know whether to sink or get butterflies. This might mean Jaz is gay, but if so, it probably also means she has a crush on whoever Emma Bissett is. I'm going to lose my mind from all the not knowing.

Jaz pulls out her phone and begins scrolling, face scrunched up in a pout. I watch with bated breath. It sure takes a while. This lady must post a *lot*.

We're interrupted by a shout from the front of the bus. "We're here!"

"Oh, thank god." Jaz throws her phone back into her bag.

The rest of the bus cheers. Out the window, I see a sign that reads "Arrowhead Camp."

The energy in the air is electric—I can tell a lot of people have been looking forward to this week for the entire summer. I keep it cool, but a little bit of the excitement rubs off on me. We pile off the bus and grab our stuff from the trailer. Michael leads everyone up the path to a lodge-type building, quaint as can be, with long wood beams stained dark brown and a set of deer antlers over the entrance.

"Girls on this floor, boys upstairs. Corbin, you do you," he says, fist-bumping the genderfluid color guard captain.

We split from Emilio and Matty, who's still wearing Jaz's shirt, stomach poking out like Winnie the Pooh. Jaz leads the way, pushing Alyssa's wheelchair. They peek into the first room, which has two bunk beds, a basic dorm-style desk, and two dressers.

"Don't worry about me," Madison declares, already continuing down the hall. "I promised my sister I'd room with her."

"Perfect. Then it's me, Carina, Alyssa, and Kendall."

My heart jumps to my throat at the thought of sharing a room with Jaz for a week. "You don't have to put me in with you. I'm sure you have other friends—"

"Nope!" she says. "You're the new kid and we've taken you under our wing. Stop fighting it."

Never in my life have I encountered someone as aggressively inclusive as this woman. It would be obnoxious if she weren't, well . . . *Jaz.*

We pile into the room. Jaz and Carina immediately claim top bunks. I think about taking the bottom bunk opposite Jaz's, but then realize I can see her in bed from that angle. Not about to take the risk of me going all Edward Cullen and watching her sleep. I claim the spot beneath her and throw my duffel on the bed.

Jaz settles in above me and groans. "I forgot how terrible these mattresses are."

"Yeah, but at least we have a freaky fox to keep us company." Alyssa snorts, pointing at the back of the door. It is, in fact, decorated with a weird mural of a fox, with big eyes that are probably supposed to be cute but are actually kind of terrifying.

Jaz's bed creaks as she sits up. "Oh my god, yes. This is the best. We need to name him."

"How about Michael?" Carina suggests.

Jaz snickers. "You and your crush."

"It's not my fault!" Carina protests. "I can't resist his golden retriever energy."

"Amen," Alyssa says.

"Naw, naming it Michael is too weird," Jaz says. "How about Dr. Beat?" Dr. Beat is the loud, incessant metronome that we use to keep time in marching practice. "Or Ned?"

"Ned? Why Ned?" Alyssa asks.

"I don't know. He just looks like a Ned."

"I like it," Alyssa says. "Say hello to Ned the terrifying fox painting."

"I feel like we should pray to him or something," Carina says. "Ned is probably an elder god."

"You're right!" Jaz hops off the bed, landing next to me with a gentle thud. "Rally the troops."

"Don't we have practice soon?" I say. "The schedule said 11:00."

"Exactly." Jaz taps her chin and wanders out into the hall. She raises her voice to shout, "Everybody! New band girls tradition forming! Get over here."

I sit back and watch people obediently shuffle into our room, murmuring with confusion but still obeying Jaz's directions. I've noticed she has that effect on the people—they can't seem to help doing what she says. She's already used her powers on me more than once.

"Okay, people, meet Ned the Fox." Jaz is lit up and in her element. "Ned is an elder god who blesses bands with perfect technique and memorization. All we have to do is make sure everyone touches Ned's head before practice every morning. You all hear?"

"Sure, Jaz."

"Whatever you say, Jaz."

"We stan Ned the Fox!"

"All hail Ned!"

Everyone laughs and comes inside to pat the painting before shuffling off to gather their things for our first morning of practice. I slather sunscreen over my still-peeling burn from last week, fill my half-gallon Nalgene, and join the rest of the group on their way to the practice field.

We've beaten most of the guys, so we hurry to claim the small amount of shade for ourselves. Despite being in a forest, this part of the camp has no trees, just a small set of bleachers where we throw our water bottles and phones and sweat towels. By the markings, the clearing looks like it's usually used for soccer, but someone's placed cones and flags to outline the front half of a football field. Our band is small enough that our show probably won't even need to use the backfield, anyway.

Most of the band is ready and waiting by the time the last few members show up. A couple of underclassmen jog over after Miss Alvarez has already gathered us for announcements.

She checks her watch. "Give me two laps, Garrett and Sam, thank you. The rest of you—lunch is at 1:00, so we've got to keep this rehearsal snappy. I know you're all excited to be here, but time is of the essence. Show up on time, stay quiet, and listen to your leaders. That includes a few guests who'll be helping out this week."

Two people I don't recognize are standing next to our director. There's a short girl in a DCI tank top that shows off a hardcore tan line, and another, slightly taller girl wearing a furry trapper hat despite the temperature being almost ninety degrees.

Alvarez gestures to the pair. "Most of you already know them, but these are Hannah and Morgan. They've come to help out at camp before they head to college. Hannah was drum major for two years and plays mellophone. She'll be leading the wind section with me. Morgan was our pit captain last year, so she'll help out percussion along with our regular tech, Zach. I trust you'll all pay attention to them *just like you do to the rest of the adults.*"

By all the waving and squealing that's happening, it does seem like everyone knows these girls well. Jaz gives the first one, Hannah, a big hug while simultaneously high-fiving Morgan. I hang back while the reunions go on for at least a minute. Alvarez, surprisingly, lets it happen.

"Let's get started," Michael finally calls with a clap of his hands. "You should all have your dot books complete by now. Did anyone, God forbid, leave theirs at home?"

I pull out my notebook, which I've looped through some string to wear around my neck during rehearsal. I wasn't about to risk more attention by forgetting it this time.

The boys who were late have just finished their laps. Panting, one of them raises his hand. "I swear I thought I had it . . . ."

Michael wails an exasperated, "Garrett!" and several people echo him. "Ugh, Garrett!"

Garrett puts his hand in his pocket and produces a small notepad. "Just kidding! Got you guys."

Everyone takes another round of yelling at Garrett while we head out onto the field. Michael guides us into an evenly spaced block for some marching technique. I'm a good instrumentalist—I kind of have to be, as a Mathis—but marching sometimes gives me trouble. Especially because I've had to learn three separate bands' styles. I'm all focus as Michael works us through drills, matching the height of my steps and the roll of my foot to everyone else's. The sun peaks and sweat starts to drip down my back, but I don't pay attention. I'm not about to call attention to myself by being the weak point in the band.

I end up next to Madison, our section leader, during a water break. She has sparkly blue nail polish on, a freckled face that she keeps makeup-free, and an overall vibe that tells me she might be the person to ask for band gossip. I've been wondering about Jaz's dare on the bus all morning.

"Hey." There, nice and casual.

Madison quirks an eyebrow at me as she takes a swig from her trendy, stainless steel tumbler.

I am so, so bad at being nonchalant, but I have to know. "I had a question for you. You know that girl you guys were talking about during Truth or Dare? Emma something. I was just curious . . . who is she?"

"Oh, Emma Bissett?" Madison grins and taps her fingers on the sides of her tumbler. "She's Jaz's ex-girlfriend. They're both on the track and field team. Emma pole vaults and Jaz is probably the best sprinter in the district. They dated a few years back, but it ended badly. They hate each other now."

Okay, so that could be good. It at least tells me Jaz is definitely into girls. But hate can mean a lot of things. I'm surprised by how stressed I am at the idea of Jaz having feelings for someone else. It's like I've somehow made her out to be "mine" in my brain without even realizing it. I chew myself out—*Jaz is* not *yours, and she isn't going to be. You're not gonna catch feelings for* anybody, *much less someone so amazing and cute and funny and—*

Well, shoot.

We work on the drum break outside after lunch, holding our instruments but not playing. Michael and the guest tech, Hannah, guide us through some choreography to keep us busy while the percussionists do their thing. It's still sweltering outside, and I'm in a bad mood. It doesn't help that Jaz is back to her sports bra. With her carrier and snare on, there's not quite as much skin, but it's hard not to stare at her back while we do stupid interpretive dance moves with the color guard. Miss Alvarez has Jaz playing the drum feature on her own, since she's already memorized it.

I'm hypnotized by the way the muscles in her back tense and flex as she plays. And she's good. *Really* good. One week into band and she has it down with zero flaws. It's unfair how everything comes easily to Jaz—she's apparently a track star, everyone likes her, and now I find out she's some kind of musical prodigy as well. Figures.

***

AT DINNER THAT evening, Jaz has thankfully showered and changed into a baseball tee and leggings. I wasn't going to survive if she went around in her sports bra and shorts all day.

The mess hall is a big, echoey room with a kitchen and counter at the front and a projector screen at the back. A slideshow runs through snaps from the bus ride and day on the field, set to the type of bubbly pop music Caylee loves. I show up in a grand total of one photo so far: lurking in the background of a color guard group selfie, sucking a reed, unaware I've been photographed.

Oof.

I sit down with my tray next to Matty Labiche, unable to tear my eyes from the projector screen.

"Hey," he says.

"Hey."

A photo pops up that shows one of the marimba players in the pit. It's taken from a low angle, the player's mallets a blur, a single cymbal in the foreground taking up a third of the shot.

"That's a cool picture." Maybe I'm feeling lonely, embarrassed by the color guard photo bomb. I want to make small talk for once—sue me. "The framing is kind of artistic."

Matty pauses with a piece of garlic bread halfway to his mouth and smiles. "Thanks! I took it."

"Wow." I'm genuinely impressed. I'd kind of gotten the feeling Matty was a himbo—tall, nice, but not much going on in the ol' noggin. "You're a man of hidden talents."

"Hi, Kendall!" Adam plops into the seat across from me, saxophone neck strap still dangling on his chest. It dips into his spaghetti as he gets settled. "Did you hear there's cheesecake for dessert? I hope they have chocolate."

"You've got—" I gesture to the entirety of Adam's front.

He looks down. "Oops! Forgot to put that away with the rest of my instrument." He dabs at the sauce with a napkin, transferring it from the neck strap to his shirt. "Darn it!"

I affectionately watch him struggle, almost missing the next photo on the slideshow—Jaz in her pink sports bra, mugging for the camera with Carina. *Almost.*

Jaz herself is several seats down from me, far enough away that I can focus on my meatless spaghetti and Adam and Matty's conversation about video games. The two make a funny pair: a scrawny freshman with a marinara-splattered shirt and a six-foot junior looking like a curly-haired Rambo in a tie-dye bandana. Matty's sleeves have been cut off with what I can only imagine was a rusty pair of scissors, showing off biceps that I've recently learned are from competitive swimming.

Mismatched as they are, the two chatter like they're best buds. They apparently both have the gift of easy conversation, something I've never been blessed with. I've played a few of the video games they're talking about. I force myself to chip in with my opinion a few times, and they go with the flow.

The food is surprisingly decent, and there's a pleasant ache in my muscles telling me I've finished a day of hard work. I find I'm actually looking forward to my lumpy mattress in the lodge. As we finish our meal and people start heading out, I pull up the day's schedule on my phone.

I grimace. My mattress will have to wait. "'Band Bonding?' Please tell me that's not required."

Jaz materializes to lean over my shoulder and tap the top of the screen. A disclaimer in red reads, "ALL ACTIVITIES ARE MANDATORY. ATTENDANCE WILL BE TAKEN."

"This is the best part of band camp, Kendall!" She bumps my shoulder with her hip. "Silly games, getting to know each other, vulnerability. . . . You'll *love* it."

I do *not* appreciate the sarcasm.

CHAPTER FOUR

BAND BONDING TAKES place in the same building as the mess hall. We enter to an ominous scene: a large circle of folding chairs at the center of a half-sized basketball court. The floor is this flat, pink carpet that must give the absolute worst rug burns, and the brick walls are softened by thick layers of peeling paint. A half-deflated balloon bops gently in the airflow from a large ceiling fan, an out-of-reach remnant from whomever occupied this camp before us.

The color guard captain stands at the doorway and makes a tick on a clipboard as each of us enters. Gavin and Jaz stand at the center of the circle, hands clasped behind their backs like soldiers at ease.

I sit next to Adam, who is apparently having the best day of his life. His older sisters have been talking up band camp since he was little, and now he's here in the thick of it.

"Today has been *dope,*" Adam says. "I've never gotten so sweaty in my whole life. I could barely hold onto my instrument because I was sweating so bad. And I got this cool scratch from tripping over Sam during marching practice."

He lifts up his shirt to show a red line that goes from his hip to his armpit.

"Holy smokes, Adam!" I say. "That's really big. Why didn't you say anything? You should go to the camp nurse."

He shakes his head, grinning. "It doesn't hurt. Nothing'll happen unless it gets infected." He says it like the idea is absolutely thrilling.

"You're nuts," I say.

"Thanks!" he says. "Jaz tells me that all the time, but I just think I'm fun."

I smile despite myself. "I think you're fun, too."

The chairs fill up, and I don't realize I've been looking around for leaders until Gavin calls the group to order. Not even the visiting college students are here. God help us all.

"All right, for the rookies, this is Band Bonding," Gavin explains. "There are no adults allowed, because this is a special time for us to connect as a group. I am in charge, along with Jaz and Corbin. You have to do whatever we say." He rubs his hands together like a James Bond villain. "These games are meant to get you out of your comfort zone. If you're feeling awkward, that's the point. As a band, there are going to be a lot of uncomfortable moments. Bad shows, interacting with football players, tripping during a show, all that. But if we learn to work through those and support each other, we'll be unstoppable. Everybody ready?"

The group cheers. I half-raise my fist in vague support. "Woo."

Jaz steps forward. "First we'll divide into groups. To mix everyone up, I'll start with Elizabeth and have you count off, one to six."

I end up in a group with Jaz and a bunch of people

I don't know, because of course I do. We pull our chairs beneath a basketball hoop that looks like it's seen at least one of the world wars. At Jaz's instruction, we play the game where we go around and say something we'd bring to a picnic that starts with the first letter of our name.

The person to her left starts. "I'm Brayden and I'm going to bring bread."

Thrilling.

The next person has to say what Brayden's bringing as well as something that goes with their own name. I've played this game eight million times, and I always say the same thing for myself: kimchi. Because what the heck else starts with K? Nothing cool, that's what.

Jaz is last in line. She repeats everyone's picnic foods so flawlessly that I'm pretty sure she put herself at the end to show off.

I roll my eyes. "Show-off."

She tucks her hands beneath her chin and flutters her lashes, unashamed.

The next activity is introduced by Corbin.

"We're bringing this one back from last year," they say. "Everyone hated it at first, but I feel like it had the biggest effect on the group in general. After getting so vulnerable together, you'll be surprised by how close you feel to your bandmates. That's right . . . we're doing sixty seconds of eye contact."

The entire room groans, and my pulse picks up tempo. This game sounds like my own personal hell.

"Choose a partner from your group," Corbin instructs. "You'll get more out of it if it's a person you don't know very well. Sit across from them, and when I start the timer, you must look into their eyes for a full minute. Yes, blinking is allowed. No, talking is *not* allowed. Rule-breakers will be forced to run laps tomorrow."

Jaz immediately turns to me.

"Noooo no no no," I protest. "I am *not* doing this."

Wordlessly, she jerks a finger up to point at a sign I hadn't noticed on the wall behind her: "ALL ACTIVITIES ARE MANDATORY. NO EXCUSES."

Internally, I scream in frustration. Externally, I say, "Fine. But don't make it weird."

I scoot my chair to face Jaz, then Corbin starts the timer.

Our eyes meet. I clench my teeth, trying to look past Jaz like she's transparent. But I start to get a headache, and my eyes have to focus eventually. There she is, zen as can be, a relaxed smirk on her face.

She stares at me. I stare back.

Now that I'm looking, I can't stop myself from noticing every detail about her eyes. They're round and slightly downturned, with naturally long lashes. Her irises are such a deep brown they almost match her pupils. Jaz must have cleaned off her makeup during her pre-dinner shower, but she missed a smudge of mascara on her left lower lid.

I don't realize I'm biting my lip until Jaz mirrors me. My gaze darts between her mouth and her eyes, my heartbeat suddenly two hundred beats per minute.

"Time's up."

I turn away from Jaz with a gasp for air, like I've come up to the surface after being underwater. The rest of the room is giggling and talking loudly, obviously relieved to reach the end of this exercise. But my heart won't settle down. My breathing is too loud. I can't bring myself to look in Jaz's direction again. I yank my chair to face the middle of the circle, waiting until the next game is introduced.

***

DJ JAZZY JEFF 9:28 PM
Are you avoiding me?

The text pops up as I'm lying in bed that night, trying not to think about the girl four feet above me. I'm briefly confused, but then I remember that's how Jaz saved her number in my phone when she sent the UFO videos on the bus.

Kendall 9:28 PM
I'm not avoiding you

I absolutely am. I got ready for bed as quickly as possible and holed myself up in my bunk, staring at my phone with earbuds in. Jaz took her time, chatting with Carina and Alyssa as she massaged oils into her hair and tied it up with a silk scarf. Her pajamas are a simple camisole and gym shorts. She uses an electric toothbrush.

DJ Jazzy Jeff 9:29 PM
Uh-huh. Sure.

Kendall 9:29 PM
Ok maybe a little

Above me, there's a sound like the one I make when I read something funny online, a single puff of air through the nose. A nose-laugh? Is that a thing?

DJ Jazzy Jeff 9:29 PM

I wish you'd just let me be your friend, Mathis.

There it is again. Adam had said something similar on my first day: *You're really determined not to be my friend, aren't you?* I wouldn't be surprised if their parents and cousins and aunts and uncles said it to me if I ever met them.

Not that I'm hoping to meet the Whitaker family.

I sigh audibly for her benefit.

Kendall 9:31 PM
I don't NOT want to be friends with you
I just
Idk
Doesn't really make sense when I move so much. It's easier to just . . . not

DJ Jazzy Jeff 9:31 PM
What about dating? Have you ever dated someone? (Guy, girl? Idk what you're into.)

Kendall 9:31 PM
. . . .
I'm bi, so I'm into both. Just fyi
And . . . kinda. Nothing serious. Again, moving a lot. I don't really do relationships.

She doesn't reply for what feels like forever. I stare at the bottom of her bed, wishing I had whatever kind of X-ray vision would allow me to see the expression on her face right now.

DJ Jazzy Jeff 9:33 PM
What do you mean when you say nothing

serious?

Kendall 9:33 PM
  I don't know, Jazzy Jeff! Like, makeouts and stuff!
  Why am I telling you all of thisss

DJ Jazzy Jeff 9:33 PM
  I have that effect on people
  Like friends with benefits?

Kendall 9:34 PM
  Something like that. Why? You interested?

I type it without thinking, possessed by some sort of demon that makes people overly confident and flirty. But I don't mean to hit send. I don't even *remember* hitting send.

But there it is, definitely sent.

I meant it to be kind of an offhand joke, but over text, it looks a lot like a proposition. Jaz is silent above me, and three blinking dots appear and disappear half a dozen times. I am *dying*. There are so many thoughts and feelings in my head that I feel like it might explode.

I should text something else, make it clear I was joking. Unless . . . ? No, I should clarify. But now it's been so long. She'll think I meant it but chickened out. There's no getting out of this. I close my messages and open TikTok to distract myself from the doom spiral currently happening in my brain. *Scroll, scroll, don't freak out, scroll, don't freak out.*

I start to wonder if Jaz has fallen asleep, but finally, a new text appears. I tap it before my brain even registers it's there.

DJ Jazzy Jeff 9:42 PM
Can't say I'm not tempted

I swear my heart stops.
Another text, quickly after the first:

DJ Jazzy Jeff 9:42 PM
But unfortunately, I'm more of a relationship person. Old-fashioned like that.
Did you really not have friends at your old schools?

I take the conversational detour like my life depends on it. My cheeks burn, though I'm not sure whether it's with relief or disappointment. A brief image of what it'd be like to kiss Jaz flashed through my mind in that moment after the first text. Now that I've had the thought, I don't know if I'll ever be able to get it out of my head.

CHAPTER FIVE

KENDALL 7:28 AM

Morning, Pops! About to start day 2 of torture. JK it's been good. How are you/Oma/Opa?

Dad 11:55 AM
Good.

I stare at my phone. It's not like Dad to text one-word replies, and it took him hours to respond. My father is a quiet dude, but he's pretty text-savvy. He gave a similar response yesterday when I asked him if everybody missed me: "Yep." With nothing else added on.

I hate to go there, but I immediately worry his depression's worse again. He's been so much better since we got here, but that doesn't mean it can't come back. Those days after we caught Mom cheating were the worst. I could barely get him out of his room, even to eat. He started losing weight. Mom was staying in a hotel room, so Jackson and I had to figure out how to keep everybody eating more than cereal and Pop-Tarts. We watched a lot of YouTube cooking videos. Luckily, Jackson turned out to be a natural in the kitchen. He took over most of the meals, and I focused on coaxing Dad out of the darkness.

We got there, little by little. Enough for him to decide that, after the divorce was finalized, he'd head to Minnesota for a while to get some support from his parents. He said he didn't want to be a "burden on his kids." It broke my heart to hear him talk like that, and I knew in that moment I'd be going with him. At first, Mom tried to convince me I shouldn't interrupt my education, but I reminded her that her consulting job had forced us to do that every few years anyway. I was used to it.

The court allowed it—Caylee and Jackson would stay at their schools and live with Mom, but I was old enough to have a say in where I went. Unlike me, my little siblings had formed tight friend groups in Colorado they didn't want to leave behind.

Miss Alvarez's voice on the microphone jolts me from my thoughts. We're on a water break, and I'm lying under a tree with the rest of the sax section.

"Time to get back out there," Madison says, jumping to her feet and extending her hands to help Adam and Jake up.

"One sec." I fire off a quick reply to Dad.

Kendall 11:59 AM
Can we talk later tonight? On the phone?

He replies with a single thumbs-up emoji. I take a deep breath, but it does nothing for the rubber band ball of stress growing in my chest. *Shake it off, Mathis.* I pocket my phone and follow the saxes back onto the field.

***

"I'VE MADE A huge mistake." Carina winces as the camp nurse applies more aloe vera on her shoulders. "Shi—I mean *darn,* that's cold."

She smiles innocently up at Michael, who has been tasked with escorting those of us who got sunburned to a tiny cabin with a sign that reads "Health Lodge" above the door.

Our marching tech just smiles and shakes his head. "It never ceases to surprise me that with *all* the reminders, *all* the sunscreen breaks, you little gremlins still manage to get burned. Happens every year."

"To be fair, *my* sunburn was Adam's fault," I point out.

"Hey!" Adam protests.

I made the mistake today of trusting the boy to re-apply sunscreen to the lower part of my shoulder blades, where I couldn't quite reach. He missed a fist-sized spot on the left side, so I had to take the walk of shame to get treated by the nurse at the end of the day. Adam accompanied me out of guilt.

"I'm messing with you," I say. "At least I'm not as bad as Carina."

My German genes are doing me no favors, but Jaz's fair-skinned best friend is so red she's painful to look at.

"Shut up," Carina grouses. "I'm not usually outside this much. It doesn't fit my *aesthetic.*"

"Aesthetics aside, Miss Fergesen, you've got to start reapplying every hour," Michael says. "You are going to be deeply unhappy with yourself when you put on your drum carrier tomorrow morning."

"Okay, Mom," she replies in a sing-song voice.

Michael grins and shakes his head. I've already gotten my aloe, so Adam and I are picking at a puzzle someone started on the side table next to Carina's chair. She and I may not be best friends anytime soon, but I feel like I should stick around till she's done out of solidarity.

There's no box to show the completed puzzle, and the pieces are tiny. I have managed to place approximately one of them.

"This puzzle is the worst." I squint at the piece in my hand. "Does this look like part of the trees? Or the bottom of some kind of Army tank?"

"That's a streetlight," Adam says, taking it from me and placing in the exact right place, first try. "You can tell by the lighting."

I make a face at Michael. "Can you believe this kid?"

Adam shrugs. "What can I say? I like puzzles. I have a million at home. Maybe if you practiced more, you'd get a little better."

"Maybe a *little*," I grumble.

"There you go," the nurse says to Carina. "All set. I'll send you with more to apply before bed. And tomorrow, be sure you're using SPF 70 or higher. We have some for sale in the canteen if you need it."

Michael heads off to go do leaderly things, and the rest of us walk toward the trailer. A giant version of our hawk-and-velociraptor logo is emblazoned on the side in blue and gold. Band parents mill around with measuring tapes and clothes hangers, helping everyone get fit for their uniforms. I pull out my phone on our way over and see I have three missed calls from Dad.

I forgot about our talk!

"Gotta go." I split off from Carina and Adam before they even have time to reply. I dial while speed-walking around the corner of one of the main buildings.

"Come on, connect," I urge when the ring doesn't immediately start. "Stupid thing."

I wander a path that leads to a lake, phone in the air as I search for signal. Halfway down, I get some bars and the call goes through.

"Hey, Kendall! Thought you forgot about me."

I don't realize how tense I've been until relief floods through me at the sound of his cheerful voice.

"Hey, Dad. You sound like you're in a good mood."

"Opa's got bee sting cake in the oven, so it's hard not to be."

"Jealous!" My grandfather's signature dessert is filled with custard and has this sweet almond topping that I drool just thinking about. I have no idea why it's called bee sting cake, but the stuff's so delicious no one ever questions it. "So . . . you're doing okay?"

"Yes, I'm okay now, kiddo." Dad sounds apologetic. "I missed my meds yesterday, and you know how that throws me off for a while."

"Dad!" I chastise. "You promised you'd be on top of that."

"I know, I know. I'm going to do better, promise. Oma says she'll check to make sure I take them from now on. And I have cake on the way, so. . . ."

He says it like, *It's all good! Cake makes up for everything!* But I'm not letting this go so easily. I'm away for two days and he's already had an episode. Not to mention the fact that I forgot to call him because I was too busy with Adam and Carina. I can't believe myself.

I set my shoulders. "I'm going to call you after dinner the rest of the days I'm gone. And you better text me back faster, or else I'll worry. Got it?"

"Got it. But don't think about me too much while you're out there. You've got lots of fun to have."

"No time for fun. I'm focused on catching up so I'm not as bad as the freshmen anymore. It's embarrassing, honestly."

"I'm sure you're doing great," Dad says. In the background, a timer starts going off. "Gotta go! This cake's not gonna eat itself. Promise me you'll cut loose a bit?"

"Sure. Footloose," I deadpan. "Kick off my Sunday shoes."

"That's my girl."

CHAPTER SIX

DESPITE MY PROMISE to Dad, I'm the first one in bed again that night. I'm in a black tank and sweatpants, wishing I'd packed something cute. Since apparently I'm keeping track, Jaz is in a matching crop top and shorts set covered in cartoon tacos. I at least make an effort to chat with my roomies as they prepare for bed instead of putting in my earbuds. The discussion centers around tactics for tomorrow afternoon's water balloon fight. Like every other Itaska tradition I've experienced so far, people take this very seriously and have lots to say about what happened in years past. I chime in, but it's hard to get excited when I don't know half the names they mention.

Finally, everyone climbs into their squeaky bunks and settles in for the night. The quiet is punctuated only once by a giggle fit when we hear one of the boys in the room above us yell, "GIVE ME BACK MY UNICORN!" Slowly, the only sound in the room becomes the even breathing of sleep.

Then there's me, still awake, reading the Sharpie graffiti on the slats above me. Natalie and Bo are in love (good for them) and Patrick apparently eats scabs (gross). I lie there and try not to feel guilty about missing Dad's calls tonight. At least he got out of his funk. I won't always be around to check on him, especially once I go off to college, and he's made a lot of progress toward stability in a few short months. Still, it's hard not to feel overprotective. I try to remind myself that he has a psychologist and a therapist and my grandparents. I'm not alone as his sole support.

What would happen if I just let myself be a regular teenager? I'd get excited for a water balloon fight, maybe plot out how to win. I'd take a long time to respond to texts from my Dad instead of the other way around. I'd daydream about the cute girl in the taco pajamas sleeping above me, a girl who has shamelessly flirted with me more than once, who's straight-up said she's tempted to be friends with benefits.

I want to scream into my pillow. What do I *do* with this? Shiny, bubbly Jasmine Whitaker is 100% *not* part of the plan. But I've gotten caught up in this swirl of energy that always seems to be around her, and it makes me feel like things could be different, like *I* could be different.

I need fresh air. I shift to get up and my bed groans. When no one wakes, I roll off the rest of the way, cringing at how loud the bedsprings are. The wood floor is cold and smooth against my hands. I crawl to my duffel, trying to avoid the eyes of the fox-slash-Elder-God as I put on a hoodie and slides. *Don't judge me, Ned.* I slip out the door.

Arrowhead Camp is usually used for Scout troops. Wooden arrows on posts point toward archery ranges, volleyball courts, and ropes courses. Jackson did Scouts for a couple years, but he quit last year because his Colorado friends were too cool for camping and community service. My dad still invited the local troop members over to work on their automotive maintenance merit badges, and he had me assist as they took apart one of his project cars and discussed the parts that made up an engine. He gets so into that stuff, and it always makes me happy to see him happy.

This was right around when Mom started cheating, though neither of us would discover her for months. It was some guy from work with an extremely stereotypical name like Chad or Thad or something. I never bothered to learn, and he got himself out of the picture *real* quick. It wasn't about him, anyway. It all comes down to Mom and her selfishness.

I walk without a destination in mind, hoping the cool air and cricket song will settle my thoughts. I end up following the same lake path I was on earlier that day. One of the things I like most about Minnesota so far is how much water there is: rivers, streams, ponds, and *lakes*. Lakes everywhere. I swear half the kids in band live on some type of waterfront property or own boats or go to a cabin "up north" on a lake during the summer.

I wonder if Jaz lives on a lake or has a family cabin. I wonder a lot of things about her life at home. Are her parents together? What does she do for fun? How does she decorate her bedroom? My cheeks warm. I push the thoughts away, but they come back just as quickly. My brain is a traitor.

Scratching my arm, I make my way to a large log set on its side near the shore of the lake. It's smooth from years of Scouts making it their bench, and I take a seat. My arm itches again. I brush my thumb over a bump near my wrist and realize I've committed the ultimate sin—I'm out here without bug repellent. My clothes cover my arms and legs, but the mosquitoes have managed to find every bit of skin that's showing. My hands, ankles, face, and neck are all under attack. I swear and slap at them, but like the thoughts of Jaz, they keep coming back.

I scowl at the moon reflected in the still, gray waters of the lake. So much for getting some air. *I give up.*

Halfway up the trail, I hear footsteps crunching toward me. A stray flashlight beam passes over the trees to my left. I dive the other way. I suck in my stomach, trying to hide behind the trunk of a scraggly pine tree. My pulse goes into double time. Have I been discovered out of bed past curfew? Is some couple on their way to make out while I'm trapped ten feet away? I'm honestly not sure which is worse.

The figure steps into a beam of moonlight, and my fists unclench.

"Jaz?" I emerge from behind the tree. "What are you doing?"

She screams at the sight of me appearing out of nowhere. Seeing who it is, she plants her hands on her knees, half-giggling, half-hyperventilating. "You scared me."

"I can see that. Sorry."

She straightens and pats her hair, expression obscured again by the darkness. "I saw you leave the room and thought I should check on you. Is something wrong?"

Her concern stabs at my heart a little bit. "No, I'm fine. Just couldn't sleep."

"You must be getting eaten alive out here." She

pulls a travel-sized bottle of bug spray from her jacket pocket. "I figured you weren't a native, so you didn't anticipate it. Want some?"

"Oh, thank god."

We spray ourselves down. Then, without speaking, we move back toward the lake. A breeze picks up, pushing gentle waves against the shore at the base of the log. I take a seat, and Jaz plants herself a few feet down from me. Her hair is bundled up in a lavender scarf that shines in the moonlight. It looks soft.

"Do you wanna talk about it?" Jaz's voice has none of her usual directness, quiet and unsure.

I shake my head. I'm not going to burden her with my stupid family drama. And what's the other option? Tell her I've been thinking about her since we met, and it freaks me out? Admit that the image of her in a sports bra is burned into my disaster bisexual brain?

"That's fine," she says, and it sounds like she means it. "Do you want *me* to talk or just be quiet?"

"You can talk." I stare at the lake instead of her.

"Mmkay." She hugs her legs to her chest, looking out at the water, too. Something small falls from a tree down the shore, sending ripples across the smooth surface. "Thanks for being nice to Adam. I know he can be a lot."

I shrug. "The kid's growing on me."

"Well, he can't stop talking about you," Jaz says. "I don't know if he's told you, but he has ADHD. It took a while for him to get diagnosed. Our mom and dad used to get so frustrated with him. Thought he wasn't trying hard enough in school, when I knew he stressed about it all the time. Things are better now, but I still feel kind of protective."

I can tell that in thanking me, she's also warning

me. *Hurt my brother's feelings, and I'll make you regret it.*

I want to tell her I feel kind of protective about him, too. That I have a little brother three states away, and doing that puzzle with Adam today reminded me of working on the huge LEGO sets Jackson saves his lawn-mowing money to buy. None of his school friends know that we'd spend weeks after school working on one of those things. Caylee would help out sometimes, but usually it was just Jackson and me.

I wonder if he's still building them now that I'm gone.

Instead of all that, I simply say, "Adam's a good kid."

"Yeah, I like him." Jaz bumps my shoulder with hers. "Don't tell *him* that, though."

She talks some more about her family. Her mom's an accountant and her dad does construction. She has two siblings, like me, but she's in the middle. Her older sister goes to college in Pennsylvania. Her family likes to play board games together, and at least according to Jaz, she always wins at *Ticket to Ride.*

"I'm honestly surprised," I comment. "You have 'oldest child' energy."

"You take that back!"

I laugh. "I just mean that people look up to you. They listen when you talk. I'm kind of surprised you're not drum major, honestly."

"You're not too far off. I *used* to be."

"Why not anymore? Did you kick Miss Alvarez's dog or something?"

She lies back along the length on the log, hands behind her head, propping an ankle on her other knee. It's a pose that says "I'm chill," but I get the impression this is a capital-T Topic.

"I was assistant drum major last year with Hannah, that college student who's been helping out with the wind section. I loved it. But when this season was coming up, I realized I missed the music. I missed drumming. So I resigned, and they held auditions. Gavin ended up getting picked. He's done a good job."

She says it in a way that has me cocking my eyebrow. "But you could've done a little better, huh?"

Jaz laughs, obviously embarrassed but not denying it. "I'm tough on everybody, not just myself. It's like a compulsion for me, to evaluate people and see where they can improve."

I hum noncommittally. "What about me? Have I been evaluated?"

The song of the frogs on the lake comes into focus during her silence. The pulsing noise makes a steady rhythm, matching the beat of my heart as I wait for her answer.

"You're a tough one," Jaz finally says. "You keep to yourself, but you're not shy or insecure. It's like you're holding back a part of yourself, but I can't figure out why."

I try to interrupt, but she stops me with a lifted finger. "You're a good sax player, but it's not your passion. You're stubborn, and you don't always listen to advice, no matter how wise it may be." I know she's referring to the Pak's incident from the week before. "You eat Reese's Pieces like they're a delicacy. You have a crush on Billie Eilish."

"How do you—"

"You watch her music videos, like, every night." I want to interject that we've only been here two nights, but Jaz sits up and pins me with her stare. "You work hard. You listen to authority, even if you don't agree all the time. And you're way squishier on the inside than you let on."

I snort at that. She doesn't take the bait, just raises her eyebrows, daring me to contradict anything she's said. I study her face, words drying up. This girl has known me for a week. How does she see me so well already? It's freaky. I thought I'd done a good job of shielding my true self from everyone, yet here Jaz is, pulling back the layers. I feel exposed, and I don't like it.

I glare at her. She yawns.

Highly peeved, I slip my phone out to glance at the time. "Holy smokes, it's one in the morning. We've gotta get to bed."

"I know."

I groan as we get up and start heading back. "We're gonna be dead at practice. Why didn't you say something?"

"I don't know," she says. "I was just talking to you. It was nice." She smiles, no teeth, something intimate and only for me. I tear my eyes from her face to open the lodge door for her.

"Thanks."

We slip inside and back to our beds. I don't fall asleep for another hour.

CHAPTER SEVEN

DESPITE ALL MY efforts to be this cool, indifferent version of myself, Itaska Band Camp gets to me.

At Wednesday's water balloon fight, we're divided into teams based on section. The saxophones are absolutely horrible—a truly admirable display of un-athleticism—and I laugh so hard my abs are extra sore that night. Dinner is full of food sculptures by Matty and Adam and band gossip provided by Madison. Dad keeps up on his meds, and our calls are short and cheerful, just enough to check in and reassure each other we're doing fine. I avoid any further sunburn, thanks in part to signs that appear on the particle board walls of the lodge proclaiming things like, "Remember to protect your skin while you suffer!" with a clip art picture of a smiling bottle of sunscreen.

Without discussing it, Jaz and I keep meeting up at the lake after the others go to bed. We talk about everything and nothing, serious stuff and whatever antics the freshmen have gotten up to that day. Sometimes we just sit and look at the moon's reflection on the lake.

Jaz tells me more about her family, and she

eventually gets me to share a bit about mine, too. I tell her I live with my dad and grandparents but don't mention we run Schultz Music. I don't know why, but I still want to keep that to myself. If people in band know, what if they come to visit? The shop and the apartment are my childhood, the one place that's always the same despite the inconsistency that defines the rest of my life. The off-white tile countertops, the shag carpet in my grandparents' bedroom—they're frozen in time, the same as they've always been, and I can't just let the outside world in to stomp all over that. I try to imagine Jaz in the living room, watching game shows with Opa. It feels wrong, like forcing two puzzle pieces that don't quite fit.

But I want her to know me, if only a little bit, so I tell her about my siblings back in Colorado Springs. I tell her how Jackson is a punk but he's also really thoughtful deep down, and how Caylee has started wearing makeup and it weirds me out.

The only person I don't talk about much is Mom. Jaz doesn't push it, and I'm grateful for that.

***

"PLEASE, NED. I'M begging you. Just a few clouds."

Carina prostrates herself before the fox mural in our room. Jaz, Alyssa, and I are still grabbing what we need for our last full day of band camp. Jaz and I were up till midnight yesterday, and the lack of sleep is catching up to me. I can't quite stifle a yawn.

"Ned is a fickle god," Jaz taps the fox on her way into the hall. She's freshly showered after an early morning run, because she's apparently superhuman. I catch a whiff of cherry vanilla body wash when she brushes past. "This is the hottest, sunniest band camp in history. Garrett and Sam managed to cook a fried egg on a *tuba case* yesterday."

"Maybe we need to make a sacrifice," Carina suggests cheerily, getting up to follow the rest of us out.

"I've got *just* the little brother for that." Jaz pushes open the outside door and stops in her tracks.

Alyssa's wheelchair bumps into my leg as we cram into the doorway. "Ouch!"

She cringes. "Sorry. What's the hold-up, Whitaker?"

"Ladies," Jaz says, "do you see what I'm seeing?"

The group files outside, and together we tilt our faces skyward.

"Clouds," I breathe.

Not just a few, either. The sky is awash in light gray, cloud cover stretching to the horizon. This stuff isn't going away anytime soon. The sun is completely hidden, and the air feels cooler than it's been all week. A breeze tugs the baby hairs loose from my ponytail.

"Ned came through!" Carina fist bumps Alyssa. "I knew he would."

"Aw, no sacrificing Adam?" Jaz whines.

We trek out to the practice field. My steps are lighter and my muscles, for the first time all week, don't feel sore. Guess my body is getting used to the abuse. I'm not going to lie—I'm proud of how much progress I've made this week. I look and sound like any other senior playing out there now. And on top of everything, it's been more fun than I've had in a long, long time.

Jaz glances sidelong at me, mouth tipped up in a crooked smile.

"What?" I ask, suddenly self-conscious.

"You're starting to like us. After trying so hard not to."

I make a noise of disbelief. "Am not."

"Sure." Her eyebrows rise and lips thin in clear skepticism. "You keep telling yourself that."

Everyone is energized by the cooler weather, and our last day of practice goes better than I could have expected. Even the rookies are hitting the correct positions on the field (most of the time). Miss Alvarez claps her hands at the end of afternoon practice and gets on the mic for one final speech.

"I gotta admit," she says. "You've impressed me. It's been a long, hard week, and I think you all have the scars and tan lines to prove it. But this is miles farther along than you were at the beginning of camp. You should be proud of yourselves."

Everyone cheers at the rare praise from our director.

Now Michael takes the microphone. "Ditto to everything Alvarez said. I also wanted to give a special compliment to everyone who's new this year. You've passed the rite of initiation we call band camp, and you've done it with flying colors. I've loved seeing you all make friends and become integral parts of the band. Whether you like it or not, you're one of us now!"

More applause. Michael points directly at me and gives a triumphant thumbs up. I roll my eyes.

We're shepherded off to a banquet dinner of enchiladas and tacos, where section leaders give speeches and we watch yet another slideshow of the week's photos set to cheesy TikTok songs. Half the band's crying by the end. Awards are handed out, mostly silly ones voted on by the band, like "Worst Sunburn"—Carina, of course—and "Laziest Section," which is apparently given to the pit every year since they don't have to march like the rest of us. They accept the cardstock certificate and pose for a photo in which everyone in the section is subtly flipping the bird. The rest of the band boos them off stage.

Gavin quiets the crowd down so he can announce the next accolade. "This is a coveted one, and I know a lot of people who are deserving of it. But this year, we wanted to do something different from usual. Instead of giving this to a member who's completely new to marching band, all of us agreed this should go to someone who's just new to the Itaska High way of doing things. They've quietly worked their butt off all week, and we wanted to make sure their effort is acknowledged. Ladies and gentlefolks, let's give it up for our Rookie of the Year, Kendall Mathis!"

My mouth drops open.

I'm rooted to my seat until Jaz slugs me on the arm and shouts, "Get up there!" *God, this is embarrassing.* Attention is *literally* what I was trying to avoid by working so hard. I drag my feet on my way to the front of the room. The band is clapping, and Adam's giving a one-man standing ovation. I want to hurl myself out a window.

Finally I make it to Gavin and take the certificate. I raise it in the air, give everyone a tight smile, and hurry back to my seat. I slouch so low I'm practically under the table.

"You should've seen yourself." Jaz's eyes shine with unshed tears as she giggles. "You looked like you were contemplating murder."

"I still am."

***

"FANCY SEEING YOU here."

Even though this is our fourth night of meeting

out by the lake, we always do it the way it happened on Tuesday. After everyone else is asleep, I get up and walk along the path to sit on the overturned tree trunk by the shore. A few minutes later, Jaz shows up, dressed in sweats and bringing bug spray.

"Yes, such a surprise." I play along, making space for Jaz on my makeshift bench.

She sits, shoulder inches from mine (not that I'm noticing). She lets out a big breath, face turned to the star-filled sky. "Ah, band camp. Another one down."

"Another one down," I echo. "Was it as good as other years?"

"Honestly? Better."

I tense, hoping she won't continue. I think I know what's coming, and I really don't want her to say it.

Jaz tilts her head to give me side-eye. "What?"

"What?" I'm basically a parrot at this point.

"You got all stressed when I said that."

"No, I didn't."

"Yes, you did."

"Nuh-uh."

"*Yuh-huh.*" She pokes me in the arm. "I was going to say that band camp is better with you here. Why does that freak you out?"

God, this girl is pushy. "You're too nice to me."

"I think I'm just the right amount of nice to you. You're a cool person, and I'm glad we met. Simple as that."

My chest feels like it's on fire. How is it so easy for her to say this kind of stuff? What sort of person expresses her feelings so openly, without any fear?

"Lucky you. You get to hang with 'Rookie of the Year.'" I wave my hands, like *Woohoo, such a big deal.*

"That was hilarious," Jaz crows. "The second Gavin brought it up in our meeting, I knew you'd hate it. But everyone agreed—you busted your ass out there this week. You deserved it."

"I wouldn't have worked so hard if I'd known I'd be *recognized* for it." I shudder. "All those blisters on my feet for nothing."

"At least they're not on your hands too." Jaz holds out a palm, and I see painful-looking sores where her drumsticks rubbed against her skin.

"Dang!" I take her hand, gingerly examining the blisters. "That must hurt."

Jaz shrugs. "I'll get callouses eventually. Always do." Is it just me, or is her voice a little shaky now?

I'm still touching her. I should let it go now. Instead, I brush my thumb slowly over her palm, avoiding the sores. Silent, we stare at our hands between us, caught in a spell because we're out in the middle of nowhere, it's the last day of camp, and tomorrow we have to go back to real life. Waves lap against the sand, and the rhythm hypnotizes me. I'm using all my fingers now, fleeting touches following every line to its endpoint on her cool skin. If I stop touching her now, will the spell go away? I don't want it to end.

I glance up. Jaz still watches the subtle movement of our hands together, her eyelashes long and lowered. She swallows, a gentle motion in her jaw and throat. Now I can't stop looking at her. That spell must be what gives me the courage to reach out with my other hand and tilt her chin in my direction. It's what urges me to lean forward, gaze willing her to meet my eyes.

Jaz's breath stutters and she turns her head away from me a few degrees. My heartbeat stops in its tracks.

"I'm sorry." She gently extracts her hand, not meeting my eyes. "It's . . . not that I don't want to."

"Do you?" My voice comes out strangled, barely a gasp of a sound. I'm still tilted forward, frozen. "Want to?"

Her head bobs up and down once. "But I don't do this. Kissing people without . . . you know. Having some kind of relationship. Dating. Whatever you call it."

"Ah." My heart restarts, now beating painfully hard against my breastbone. The thing's going wild in there. "I . . . don't really . . ."

"I know," she says, cutting me off. "You don't really do relationships."

And I don't. Never really wanted to, at least until recently. Somehow, in a week and a half, Jaz has wormed her way through some crack in my armor and found a place to settle where I can't ignore her. How did she do that so quickly? And how did I let her?

I sigh. "I'm sorry. I just . . . really want to kiss you."

"Yeah." Jaz nudges at some rocks on the ground with her foot. I watch her progress as she pushes them a little farther with each slow swing of her leg. Suddenly, she sits up straight and turns to face me. "But if you could just give it a chance." She's less reserved now, more animated with every word. "Dating. I really like you, Kendall. I feel like we have this connection, and I want to explore that. Don't you? We could be good together. I know it."

A dose of panic floods my veins. This is exactly what I was scared would happen if I let someone in. She wants me to make a choice, commit, put down roots. She doesn't understand that if I do, it'll only be more pain once I uproot again. For me and for her. A wave of irritation joins the panic, and I latch onto it.

"Jaz, I don't know what else to tell you." I scrub a hand over my face. "I'm not staying in Itaska, so anything that starts between us will end before it really even begins. After this year, I'm off to Michigan for college. Or if I don't get into Michigan, somewhere else. I can't stay."

"Why not?" she challenges.

I shake my head. "The point is, Itaska is a pit stop. A place for me to wait around until I can move on with my actual life."

A flash of hurt crosses Jaz's face, but she quickly masks it. "That's my hometown you're talking about. You haven't even given it a chance. You're so determined to bide your time that you're gonna miss out on what could be the best year of your life! Sure, you'll leave for college eventually. But you're here for now. So let yourself *be* here."

This girl. So frustrating. "We're not even technically in Itaska right now."

"Itaska's like Asgard. It's not just a place. It's a bunch of cool people you seem determined not to like."

"They're not all trying to be besties with me either. I overheard Madison tell Adam he should've been Rookie of the Year instead. Carina *still* barely tolerates my existence."

"Madison is just extra. She doesn't mean anything by it. And Carina . . . is Carina. She'll come around."

"Sure."

I realize I'm still holding her hand and drop it. She narrows her eyes at me, and I narrow mine back. Then an evil smile slowly appears on her face, full-on

Grinch style.

"I have an idea."

God help me.

"If you're so determined to treat Itaska like a stepping stone to better things, that's your prerogative." She pokes me in the chest. "But I think deep down, you *want* to like it here. We've started to get to you already, and it's only been a week. So I'm going to make you a bet: I, personally, will get you to fall in love with Itaska—and everybody in it—by homecoming weekend."

"And if I don't?"

Jaz leans forward, lashes lowering. "Then I'll let you have that kiss."

CHAPTER EIGHT

I WAKE UP that morning and Jaz is already gone on her morning run. I swear the woman doesn't need sleep to function.

The bus is waiting outside after we have a quick grab-and-go breakfast, and I end up being one of the first on-board. I find a seat near the back and settle in with my AirPods. I almost start a Billie Eilish video when I remember Jaz's calling me out, so I switch to a random "New in Indie" playlist. I'm really getting into the music when I feel the cushion of my seat dip.

Jaz plucks an earbud from my ear and puts it in her own. "Oo, I like this. Who is it?" Her eyes glint with a challenge.

I half-heartedly grab for the earbud. "Give it."

She shakes her head, settling in next to me and tapping her leg in time with the music. Finally, I grab the earbud away, and she whines, "Ow! That hurt."

"Should've asked permission," I say with a smirk. "Why aren't you sitting with Carina, anyways?"

"Carina knows of my conniving schemes and fully supports them." She pulls a bag of Reese's Pieces from her drawstring backpack and waves it in front of my face. "Got you something."

"Where did you find those? The vending machine in the mess hall ran out!"

"There's one in the basement of the lodge." She opens the bag and pops one in her mouth.

Oh man, this is just playing dirty. How am I supposed to say no to Reese's Pieces? She holds out the bag. I snatch it and toss a few into my mouth, maintaining a frown in her direction the entire time. I know what she's up to—trying to get me to reconsider my stance against commitment. I guess she figures if she wiggles her way into my good graces, she'll win that bet.

"You're welcome," she says sweetly. "And now, I will leave you to your music. Because I know that's what you like, and I want you to be happy, because I care about you."

I ignore the jab and lean my head against my window, trying to ignore the sound of Jaz's voice greeting friends as everyone loads onto the bus. Her adorable laugh floats over my music, so I reach into my bag and bump the volume up until I can't hear her anymore. Then I pretend to take a nap so no one tries to get me to play Truth or Dare.

I must actually fall asleep at some point, because when I open my eyes again, we're no longer in the forested area of Arrowhead Camp but in long, straight fields of corn. The bus is quiet. Those not napping are speaking in hushed voices. I start to shift before I realize there's a weight on me. It's Jaz—she's fallen asleep on my shoulder.

I glance around, but no one's paying any attention to us. Jaz's full lips are parted, and she smells like cherry vanilla. I take a deep breath. Her body is warm and relaxed against my side. I'm pretty sure she didn't mean to be sleeping on me—a little inflatable neck pillow lies at our feet. If I move to pick it up, she might wake, so I sit there, frozen by indecision.

Madison turns around in her seat, then gets up on her knees when she realizes I'm awake. "Finally!" she whispers. "I'm surprised you slept that long. It's been really bumpy on some of these roads. Look what I got." She holds out her phone.

It's a photo of Jaz and me. Our faces are soft in sleep, our mouths curved up. We look so comfortable. If I were a stranger, I'd 100% think we were a couple. We fit together like it's the most natural thing in the world.

"I'm deleting this," I hiss.

Madison smirks. "Doesn't matter. It's in the cloud, baby!"

"You're the worst."

I must say it a little too loudly, because Jaz stirs and yawns. When she realizes we're cuddling, she sits up, and her eyes zero in on the picture.

"Creep!" She thwacks Madison on the head with her hoodie sleeve, but she doesn't make any move to grab the phone. In fact, a little smile grows on her face as she looks at the photo.

I shove my earbuds back in and turn away from both of them.

***

DAD PICKS ME up in the school parking lot. To my relief, his smile is genuine and I can't see any bags under his eyes. We've been talking every day, so I was pretty sure he was on track, but I couldn't help worrying. I've just started getting my dad back, and I don't want to lose him again.

He asks me about camp, and I decide to actually give him more of an answer than "Fine." What can I say? I'm happy to see him. I try not to mention too much about Jaz or any specific friends—don't want to get his hopes up—but I tell him about our show and the activities I did (i.e. got forced to do) at Arrowhead Camp. He eats it up.

Our drive home winds along the north bank of Whiskey River until we reach the historic downtown area of Itaska. The oak-lined main street is busy with pedestrians out to get late lunches or to visit the hip wine bar with a "Grand Opening!" sign. There's even a busker on the corner, playing acoustic guitar and wailing a song I don't recognize.

I'll admit, the whole thing is pretty dang charming. It's like the entire population of Itaska showed up to make it harder for me to win that bet with Jaz. But I want that kiss, and I'm not going to let a quaint little town get in the way of that. Who cares if a cute baby waves at me from her dad's lap in a bicycle rickshaw? Not me.

We pull into the lot behind Schultz Music next to my—*my!*—motorcycle.

"How much work do we have left on the Sportster?" I ask Dad.

He frowns at the bike. "A few hours, maybe?'

"Can we finish it this weekend? First day of school is coming up. I'd love to drive myself."

Dad grins, folding his hairy arms. "Planning to make a grand entrance?"

". . . No."

"Uh-huh," he says. "Sure."

"Dad."

He smacks me on the back. "Of course we can get it fixed up for school, kiddo. Great idea."

My grandparents both wrap me in hugs when we come in, and I relent, squeezing back tightly. I missed them while I was gone, missed Oma's quirks and Opa's calmness and the dusty cedar smell of their apartment. Opa has a lunch of pasta and iceberg salad ready on the table. The fact that they sat around waiting for my return is so wholesome I have to consciously force myself back into New Kendall mode to avoid tearing up.

"Did you make any new friends?" Oma asks as we sit down to eat.

I've already stuffed my mouth full of pasta, so I shrug and make a noncommittal grunt.

Oma looks like I just smashed a Stradivarius in front of her. "Kendall! Do not tell me you went away for a whole week and did not talk to people your entire time there."

I swallow. "I *talked* to people."

The three of them stare like I'm a sad little kitten stuck in the rain. Their pity rubs me the wrong way.

"Don't worry about me!" I say. "I had a perfectly fine time at band camp, and I'll have a perfectly fine time at school, too. Just don't expect me to host raging parties in your living room anytime soon."

After lunch, Dad and I go out back to work on the Sportster. He seems to have used up all his questions in the car, thankfully. We work in companionable silence for about an hour before my phone buzzes.

I wipe my hand on a towel and pull it out to see the call is from Mom, of all people. She hasn't communicated much since I got here, mainly texts to make sure I'm not dead or to ask for stuff. I decline the call, figuring I'll return it later, but my phone lights up once more as she tries again.

I let myself into the back door of the shop so Dad

doesn't hear me answer. "Hey, Mom."

"Kendall," she says, sweet and drawn out. I suspect she's had some wine—I've gotten pretty good at detecting that. "I wasn't sure if you would answer."

"Well, I did," I say. "What's up?"

"Just wanted to check in on my oldest daughter. How are you doing? Has school started yet?"

"Not yet. I've been at band camp, remember? I told you a couple days ago when you texted me about how to find Caylee's pointe shoes."

"That's right." She gives a little chuckle, like *silly me, my teenage daughter has her life more put together than I do.* "Well, I hope you're having a fun time out in Minnesota. I kind of miss that old apartment over the music shop. Maybe I'll come visit sometime."

"I don't think that would be a good idea, Mom."

She huffs. "Yes, well, we'll see. I miss my girl."

A vice tightens around my chest. "I miss you too, Mom."

It's true, in a complicated, twisted way. I'm furious with her, and she's been acting like a child. But she's my mother. Before this, the longest we'd been apart was for other band camps. It's weird not seeing her at the coffee pot when I come out for breakfast, not smelling her Kate Spade perfume on a trench coat hung by the door. She worked long hours, but she was a fixture in my life that's missing now.

At the same time, I know a visit from Mom would be disastrous. The divorce proceedings were relatively amicable, mostly because Dad didn't want drama. But I'm positive he would struggle seeing her. He'll need a good, long time to get his mental health under control before we contemplate any kind of family meet-up with all five of us.

Mom's going to fly me out for Thanksgiving, but as far as I know, Dad will be staying here. I miss Caylee and Jackson so much that, hopefully, seeing them will make up for any Mom drama. She's hard to handle in undiluted quantities.

"I've got to go," I say. "Talk to you later."

"Bye, sweetie."

I put my phone on silent and return to Dad.

"One of your secret new friends you don't want to admit you made at camp?"

"Something like that."

By the time we finish working for the day, I'm exhausted, sweaty, and covered in motor oil. I scrub my hands in the kitchen sink. Even with a stiff-bristled brush provided by Opa, I can't get all the black out of my hand creases. I don't mind. As a little kid, I'd sit on Dad's lap and examine every bit of his oil-stained hands. Now I'm like him.

It's been a long day. I settle down on the living room rug, too lazy to make it to the couch, and pull out my phone. There's a text from Jaz.

DJ Jazzy Jeff 4:23 PM
How's being home? Happy to see beautiful, sunny, charming Itaska again?

Kendall 5:03 PM
Terrible. Horrible. What an ugly town. And the people—degenerates. How could anyone live here?

She replies with a long string of laughing emojis. I grin at my phone, imagining that so-cute-I-could-hurl giggle. A wheezing, old-man cough makes me look up. Opa's watching me from his La-Z-Boy in the corner, looking a lot more observant than I would prefer. I forget he's there sometimes. I reset my face into a neutral expression, brows raised at him in a challenge. He smiles, shrugs, and leans back for a nap.

CHAPTER NINE

IT'S READY. AND right on time.

I stand over my bike, grinning like a madwoman. My backpack's heavy on my shoulders, packed with first-day-of-school supplies. My sax is already on the back of the seat, strapped on with a nylon bungee cord from Oma's unlimited supply of odds and ends in the shop.

"All ready?" Dad is at my side, giving the Sportster a similar look of pride and satisfaction. We put a lot of work into this thing, and now it's running smooth as butter. We deserve a little moment to be proud of ourselves.

I turn to him, hands shoved in my pockets. "Thank you so much, Dad. Seriously. This is the best present ever."

He pats my shoulder a little awkwardly. "I'm glad you like it."

I've learned not to be excited about first days of school anymore, since they tend to be disappointments. But this time, I have purpose.

Jaz says I can't kiss her until I win our bet, but homecoming weekend is over a month away. I can't wait that long. I know that if I can just get one little kiss from Jaz, I'll be able to get her out of my head and move on with the rest of my school year. Time is of the essence, and I've got a plan.

Part one of this plan? Show up to school looking like a badass. I'm going to blow Jaz's socks off.

Less badass is the fact that the marching band has to arrive early, since we'll be performing in the pep rally kick-off that Itaska apparently does every year. Miss Alvarez instructed us all to wear the school colors, blue and gold, and meet behind the fieldhouse at 7:30 sharp. I'm wearing a leather jacket over my school colors, my most flattering boyfriend jeans, and white Converse shoes. The outfit's topped off with a pair of aviators and a lipstick called "Choco Razz."

My grandparents emerge from the back door and hurry over to hug me.

"Oh, you look so cool." Oma fusses over my outfit, trying to button the top of my jacket while I dodge her.

With a big smile on his face, Opa pats my arm. Dad double checks that I have all my school supplies. Oma takes a photo of me with my backpack in front of the Sportster, like it's the first day of kindergarten and I'm the only five-year-old on the planet with a motorcycle.

"Okay, okay, I'm gonna be late," I protest, and they finally release me. I climb onto the bike and ride away.

It's overcast, and I say my prayers there won't be rain later today. It'd be a huge pain to ride home in that or, god forbid, ask someone else for a ride. For now, I appreciate the clouds since they keep me shaded in my not-quite-summer-appropriate outfit. I glance at the clock on my dash—I'm going to be cutting it close. I really don't want Alvarez to make me run laps.

I pump the gas a little more than I usually do, going six or seven miles per hour over the speed limit as I ride the already familiar route to school.

As I pass Pak's, I glance in my rearview mirror and see a police car pull out from a hidden alley. It starts to follow me, and my heart leaps into my throat. I immediately slow to the speed limit, even though I know it's too late. The cop probably already has me on their radar. Their lights go on.

Cripes. My first actual ride on this thing, and I'm about to get a ticket. Dad has always been huge on safety, ever since I got my motorcycle license at sixteen and started taking one of his extra bikes out with him. He got me all the protective gear, and I'm banned from going on the highway.

And now I've screwed it all up.

I slow down and pull to the side of the road, fingers clenching the handlebars. I feel like an idiot. Red and blue lights flash in my mirrors, growing closer and closer . . .

. . . and the cop car continues past me.

My chest heaves as I watch the cruiser disappear around a corner, off to do something that doesn't include giving me a ticket for speeding. Which I was absolutely doing. *Holy smokes. I just got very lucky.*

After I finally slow my heart, I glance at my phone. *Annnd I'm late.* Out of the frying pan and into the fire of Alvarez's wrath.

I pull into the parking lot behind school exactly one minute after we're supposed to be there. Everyone in band is waiting on the grass, milling about with their instruments. I spot Jaz chatting with Gavin by the tennis court fence. Alvarez is nowhere to be seen.

I need to remember the plan—even if I'm freaked out about tickets and doing laps, I can still make a grand entrance. Fashionably late is a thing for a reason. I roll into the parking spot closest to the tennis courts.

A few people glance over at my arrival, including Jaz. I climb off my bike and lean my hip on the seat, then I pull off my helmet with a flourish. I run my hand through my hair casually, shaking it out.

When I look at Jaz, she's frozen mid-sentence. I leave my helmet and grab my sax. I stride over to where she stands, mouth agape.

"Hey guys. How's it going?" I say.

Jaz shakes her head like a cartoon character coming out of a trance. Gavin looks between us and answers, "Good . . . ?"

I smile and push my aviators onto my head. "Great. Happy first day of school!" And okay, maybe I sway my hips a little extra as I brush past Jaz.

"Looking fly, Mathis!" Madison bumps my fist as I join the rest of the saxes and get my instrument out before Miss Alvarez can catch me.

The group buzzes with first-day-of-school excitement. Some people are quietly rehearsing the school fight song. The two Itaska High mascots, a hawk and a velociraptor, are waiting to walk in with us, but they've switched costume heads and are taking selfies. The trombones have completely ditched their instruments on the ground while they have a slap fight. Finally, Alvarez appears and shouts for everyone to line up and put their heads back on. I leave my jacket, backpack, and case against the wall of the school with everyone else's stuff.

"Remember, aside from some of the athletes and teachers, today is everyone's first day back in the building," she says. "This is the first impression the rest of the school will have of this year's Itaska Marching Band. Which is to say, don't suck."

A few people laugh. Then Gavin calls us to attention, and we snap into place.

"How are your feet?" he shouts.

"Together!" we reply in unison.

"Chest?"

"Out!"

"Shoulders?"

"Back!"

"Chin?"

"Up!"

"Eyes?"

Our volume doubles. "With pride!"

He repeats the "Eyes!" call twice more, each time our intensity increasing until we dissolve into yells and cheers on the last one.

"Let's show them who we are!" Gavin whoops and leads us into the fieldhouse.

***

THE ITASKA FIGHT song is still echoing through my head by the time lunch rolls around. I swear we played it ten times during the assembly.

I survey the food options, trying to figure out if I'll be able to keep to my Lazy Vegetarian ways at this school. There's a sad-looking salad bar, complete with those mini corn cobs nobody likes. A sign over the pizza warmer tells me there should be cheese slices, but all I see is sausage and olive. And the main entrée is Swedish meatballs, which by definition don't really work.

I've resigned myself to picking off pizza toppings when my phone buzzes with a text.

Mom 11:55 AM

Jackson got into a fight at School and got sent Home. Can you talk to him?

No "Hey, how's your first day of school in a new city?" Just a request to take care of her kid's behavior since she can't do it herself and she refuses to interact maturely with Dad. I grumble and begin composing a text to Jackson, then decide that a phone call would probably be best for something like this. Since he got sent home, he probably doesn't have much to do, but I know how good he can be at ignoring texts when he wants to.

I get out of line and find a quiet corner in the locker area, sinking to the floor so I'm out of sight of teachers.

I realize I wasn't really expecting Jackson to answer when his sullen "Hello?" throws me off guard.

"Hey, it's Kendall." I shift the phone to my other ear, not sure what to say now that I have him. "Mom told me something came up at school."

His sigh lasts a full five seconds.

"What happened?" I ask. "This isn't really like you. It must have been something big to get you throwing hands."

"I don't know. It just happened."

"Who did you fight?"

Another drawn-out sigh. "Some kid from school. Caleb. He was being a dick. I pushed him a little, then he hit me. That was it. A teacher stopped us before anything else happened."

"You got sent home for pushing someone a little?"

"Maybe it was more than a little."

Oh, Jackson. Stupid, hot-headed Jackson. "I still don't get it. You started high school like a week ago."

"You don't need to get it. It's not like you're around to help with anything. You're just talking to me because Mom made you."

His accusation stings. "I've talked to you since I left."

"Like twice."

"It was more than—" I cut myself off. Not the point. "Jackson, just because your sister doesn't call you every day, doesn't mean you should be getting into fights with some kid named Caleb! I don't know why you're trying to make this about me. You're a freshman now. You're the oldest kid at home. You need to take care of yourself."

"I'm not like you, Kendall. I don't want to forget everyone the second they're out of my sight. I actually care about people."

Oof. That one hurts.

"Whatever." I squeeze my fist to keep from sniping back at him. "You need to get yourself together, Jacks. I can't always be there to help you out of stuff now. I've got to go—lunch is ending."

"Bye." He hangs up without fanfare, leaving the conversation feeling incomplete and uncomfortable.

CHAPTER TEN

"MATHIS! HEY!"

JAZ is waving me over to her cafeteria table. Carina and Matty are with her, watching me expectantly. Matty has a French fry hanging out of his mouth.

I smile tightly and set my tray of pizza and Caesar salad next to Matty's. The only type left was supreme, so I get to work picking off the pepperoni cubes and placing them to the side. Matty snitches a couple and resumes an in-progress conversation with Carina about Marvel versus DC. These people sure love to debate.

Jaz leans over the table with a quizzical look. "Everything okay? You look grumpier than usual."

I shoot her my best death glare. "It's nothing." There's no way I'm divulging all my family drama to her.

"Come on. You can talk to me."

Irritation flares up in my chest. "I told you it's nothing. Can't you leave it alone? Go argue about Batman or something."

She recoils, looking hurt, and I immediately regret lashing out.

"I'm just having an off day," I mutter, spearing a crouton so hard my plastic fork breaks. "Goddammit."

To my dismay, Jaz follows me as I get up to retrieve a new utensil.

"I know what would make you feel better." She nods confidently. "What are you doing after school?"

"Nothing," I say, though I'd just planned an *X-Files* binge with Dad to make up for the way this day's been going. "Why?"

Jaz's mouth curls up. She's wearing some kind of pink lip tint. Idly, I wonder if it's raspberry-flavored, like mine.

"Meet us in the Cave after the bell rings. You're going to take part in a decades-old tradition."

***

I TEXT DAD to let him know I have to back out on our *X-Files* watch session. He sends three crying emojis and a thumbs down.

Kendall 12:17 PM

Are you going to be ok? Oma & Opa gonna be around?

Dad 12:18 PM

I'll be fine, K. Go have actual fun!

It's impossible to read tone over text, but at least he's not sending one-word answers. I'm 96% sure he's not about to spiral.

Kendall 12:18 PM

Text me if you need anything and I'll come right home.

When the final bell rings, I linger at my locker for a bit so I don't look too eager for whatever Jaz has planned. Staying detached is an important part of maintaining New Kendall, the girl who doesn't care about anything. I mess with my hair in the magnetic mirror I've placed inside my locker door, trying to look casual even though I'm realizing I've had helmet hair all day. I've been trying to stop using heat styling on it, but the humidity of Minnesota has made parts super wavy while others are stick-straight. Not my best look.

After five minutes, I shut my locker, shoulder my backpack, and head to the Cave. Turns out it's not a literal cave. The door at the back of the band room leads to a storage space that is apparently an all-important hangout spot for the percussionists and a few select friends in the wind section. I suppose I should be honored Jaz has invited me back there.

There are about a half-dozen other people there, mostly the regular crew of juniors and seniors from band camp—plus Adam, of course.

His head appears from behind Matty when I enter the room, and his face lights up with glee. "Kendall's here!"

He hops to his feet and skips over to me for a fist bump. After we make contact, he pulls back his hand and splays his fingers, making an explosion noise. Amused, I do the same.

"That's everybody," Jaz says, shooting me an appraising look. "Y'all ready to go?"

There are a few whoops and murmurs of assent. It seems like everyone knows what's going on but me. *Whatever.* New Kendall goes with the flow.

Jaz leads us through the school and to the front

parking lot. "We're meeting at Leghorn Park. Who can take people?"

Gavin raises his hand. "Room for three in mine."

"I've got Alyssa's mom's van," Matty says. "So we can take two others."

I raise my hand too. "I'd rather not leave my bike here. Room for one other, I guess."

I mean it as a joke, but Jaz taps her chin with one finger. "Carina, you go with Madison in Gavin's car. Emilio, Adam, you're with Matty and Alyssa. As for *me,*" she says, "I'm riding the motorcycle."

The whole room *oooh*s. Guess I can't back out now. The rest of the group wanders to their respective cars, and I lead Jaz to the Sportster with my heart pounding against my ribcage. She examines the bike with folded arms.

"This thing is safe, right?" she says. "You know what you're doing?"

There's the slightest tremble in her voice, and I realize Jaz Whitaker is scared. She may have acted like it was no big deal in front of everyone else, but this girl is legit nervous to ride a motorcycle.

"Leghorn Park's just up the river, right?" I say. "So it's a short ride. And the bike's perfectly functional, I promise. My d—" I'm about to tell her my dad's a mechanic, but I stop myself and let it hang there.

Jaz doesn't seem to notice. She makes a shaky little humming noise in the back of her throat. "Okay."

I hand her the extra helmet from the top case. She pushes it on over her bun. I'm surprised it fits—the girl's got a lot of hair. I grab my own helmet, straddle the seat, and back out of the parking spot.

"Time to get on," I say to Jaz, who's nibbling a fingernail and staring at the tires. "Come on, Whitaker, I'll take care of you."

Her gaze flits up to mine at that. Those dark eyes are wide, unsure, but I see trust there as she nods. "Let's do this."

She climbs on behind me and wraps her arms around my waist. She rests her helmet against my back as I start the engine. Her fingers clench painfully against my ribs, so I pat them in a way that I hope is comforting.

Then we're off. Jaz squeals as I accelerate. Her arms are so tight around my midsection that I can barely breathe, but I'm not about to say anything. This is the closest we've ever been. She could give me the Heimlich, and I'd say thank you.

We get onto the main road, which has a speed limit of forty (that I obey perfectly) and lots of stop lights. Gradually, Jaz's grip on me loosens, and when we look over to see Gavin's car next to us, she giggles and waves. They're head-banging to some ska song, and Carina's in the backseat with two hands in the air doing the "rock on" sign. Madison wolf whistles at us as the light goes green and they speed off. Jaz tenses, thinking I'm going to race them, but I speed up slowly, and her grip loosens.

At the next light, I turn and yell, "Want to take the scenic route?"

"Sure!"

I make a right and take her along a lane framed by bright green trees and old-fashioned street lamps. I've been wanting to ride here ever since Dad gave me the bike. It's a residential road, so there aren't many cars, and the river view is gorgeous. We meander down the winding street in silence, matching speed for a moment with a canoe paddled by two old men. They wave when they see us. Jaz waves back. We're too far to speak, but it's nice just to ride at their pace and trade smiles until the road curves away from the water.

I speed up and turn us onto the next bridge. Our new canoe besties, consummate gentlemen, tip their hats as we cross over. Jaz is still giggling by the time we double back to pull in front of a little green park by the river.

The rest of the group is already out of the cars and looking expectant. I'm once again reminded that I have no freaking idea why we're here. I pull in next to Gavin's car. Only when I've turned off the engine does Jaz's grip on me ease up. I feel her chest rise and fall, a quiet moment of relief just for her, and then she whips off her helmet and shouts, "I rode a motorcycle, bitches!"

Everybody laughs as Jaz regales them with the exciting story of our forty miles-per-hour joy ride through suburbia. I follow as the group meanders toward the riverside, where there's a wooden dock without rails that juts into the water.

"Hey, so . . ." I say to Matty. "What are we doing?"

"What, no one's told you?" He looks genuinely surprised, like he doesn't remember Jaz refusing to give details at lunch. He holds up a towel. "We're jumping in the river."

"I didn't bring a swimsuit," I protest. A thought fills me with horror. "I am *not* skinny dipping."

"Oh no no no, my sweet summer child," Madison butts in. "We're jumping in fully clothed."

I stop in the middle of the path and fold my arms. "On second thought, I'd prefer skinny dipping."

"You have to!" Jaz says, appearing at my elbow. "It's *tradition*."

There's that tradition thing again. What is up with these people? But Jaz's eyes are bright with anticipation, and she watches for my response with so much excitement that I can't say no.

"Fine," I grit out.

"YES!" Jaz throws her arms around me in the briefest of hugs, and I'm left dizzy in her aftermath as she dances around the crowd, instructing everyone how to do it.

"Get everything out of your pockets," she calls. "Don't be like Carina last year and drown your poor phone. And you're allowed to take your shoes off, but everything else stays on! It's the law!"

Carina's next to me, removing her hoop earrings and muttering, "Shouldn't have worn so much makeup. I don't know why I always forget this stupid thing."

"Got your phone out of your pocket yet?" I tease.

"Oh god, thanks for the reminder. You're a lifesaver." Her voice drips with sarcasm, but I see her slip a phone out of her pocket and lay it with her earrings when she thinks I'm not looking.

I throw my phone and keys in my bag, take off my shoes and socks, and pat myself down, trying to figure out what else to preserve. The riding jacket, definitely. No matter what Jaz says, I'm not getting that wet. I wish I'd been warned about this and brought a towel or something—looks like most everyone else got the memo on that. I watch people take off jewelry and empty pockets, then I turn to the river, suddenly anxious. It's not moving fast, but I can't see the bottom. It's a little murky. I remind myself that they do this every year and no one dies, but my heart still stutters.

"All right people, let's do this!" Jaz calls, ever the ringleader.

She herds the group toward the dock. Matty wheels

Alyssa down to the shore, scoops her into his arms, and steps out into the water, which swirls around his ankles. I feel like I might throw up.

I'm at the corner of the dock, the wood hot against my bare feet. Jaz slots herself next to me. I catalog her anklets instead of looking at the roiling water: multi-colored braids of thread, like the kind you'd make at summer camp or Girl Scouts. Her toenails are painted seafoam green, and there's a ring on her left pinky toe.

I glance back at the river and gulp.

Jaz says, "Just go with me. It's easy." Then she shouts, "Jump on one. Three! Two!" She wraps her fingers around mine, and my brain short-circuits. "One!"

I leap. Jaz's scream is the last thing I hear before cold water whooshes around me. Our hands separate as my bare toes touch squishy mud. I push off the river floor, breaking the surface and pulling in a lungful of air.

People surface around me, yelling and shivering and hollering. Jaz meets my eyes, face bright with adrenaline. For some reason she doesn't immediately splash away to be with everyone else. The two of us swim to the dock and hold on, spitting water and grinning at each other.

"Your mascara's running," Jaz says.

I laugh. "So's yours."

She reaches forward and swipes under my eyes with her thumb—first my right, then my left. My breath catches in my throat at the casual, caring action. Is it my imagination, or do her eyes dart toward my mouth? Her hand still hovers near my face; she hasn't drawn it back yet. Our toes brush together beneath the water.

"CANNONBALL!!"

We're swamped by a huge wave as Adam takes his second leap and plunges into the river. We laugh-scream, choking on the sudden deluge of water, and the moment is broken. Jaz dunks Adam, who splashes her in return, accidentally hitting Matty and Alyssa. Matty bellows in protest and leaves Alyssa clinging to the dock so he can dunk Adam, and soon everyone is laughing and splashing and I barely have time to think about how badly I wanted Jaz to kiss me just then.

CHAPTER ELEVEN

THE SCHEDULE FOR my first quarter at Itaska High is pretty basic. Pre-calc, chemistry, government, English lit. Oma and Opa set up most of it for me before we came out. The only class I chose myself is woodshop. The teacher, Ms. Reddy, is a tiny, no-nonsense lady with a neck tattoo. I'm assigned to a work table with a thin, quiet girl who introduces herself as Sarah and then doesn't speak a word to me for the rest of the week. It's the best.

After having a bit too much fun with the river-jumping tradition, I have to redouble my efforts to resist the charms of Itaska. At after-school marching band rehearsals, I keep to myself during water breaks and run through tricky bits of the show music. I sit with Jaz, Carina, and Matty at lunch, but I make it clear my weekends and evenings are booked up with schoolwork and family obligations. It's not a complete lie: to make peace with Jackson, I scheduled a video game night with him and Caylee this Saturday. Besides, New Kendall doesn't need invites to Slurpee runs or movie nights.

Jaz lets me make my excuses, which is surprising. She doesn't seem the type to give up on a bet.

Knowing her, she's probably biding her time, waiting for the right moment to strike. But after our little interlude in the river, I'll take what mercy I can get.

When I start school, Dad also begins his new job at Downing Auto. It's part-time for now, but the owner knows Opa and mentioned there's potential for it to become full-time eventually. Dad seems to enjoy the return to a routine, but—I'm ashamed to say—things do get boring when I don't have him to watch TV with.

"Why don't you come down to assist me in the shop?" Oma asks one evening when she notices me moping on the couch, not even looking at the phone in my hand. I've resorted to counting flowers on the wallpaper like the women in the depressing stories I've been reading for English homework. "I could use some help with the reorganization."

I've done a bit of work sorting the stacks inside the apartment, but I've avoided going down into Schultz Music during business hours. I'd never tell Oma this, but I'm terrified someone from school will see me and start making connections that I, Kendall Mathis, am related to the great Angelika Schultz. She's a bit of a legend in the Itaska music community, but to me she's just Oma, my quirky German grandmother. Another one of my weird protective family things, I guess.

"How about later tonight?" I suggest, but Oma immediately rejects that with a flick of her hand.

"Don't be silly, my Kendall. It's not like you are drowning in things to do right now. Look at yourself."

I'm suddenly quite aware that I'm slouched down so low my chin is on my chest and a sprinkling of Reese's Pieces crumbs is on my belly. I slide up to a regular sitting position and brush the crumbs away, feeling sheepish.

"I'll totally help you, Oma," I hedge. "But I don't super want to see kids from school, if I'm being completely honest."

That gets *her* in protective mode. She pats my cheeks with cold hands. "Oh no, my Kendall. Are the other kids not being nice? Why didn't you tell one of us? We could talk to your teachers or—"

"That's okay, you don't have to," I interrupt. "Thank you, seriously, but I don't want anyone to make it a thing."

And yes, maybe I'm lying by omission to let her think I'm being bullied or something. What else am I supposed to say? *Most of the kids are actually super welcoming, and I'm the one rejecting them?*

"Fine," she harrumphs. "But maybe sometime you can tell your friends to come and get a discount here. Half off for anyone who is nice to you."

I would rather die.

Oma tells me I can wait till six, when the store closes, to bring down the crate of polishing cloths currently on the kitchen counter. But she insists I get out of the house, so I throw on my riding jacket and take the Sportster out for a spin.

It rained this morning, and a hint of that musty smell still clings to the concrete as I idle at the intersection before the bridge where I first saw Jaz. Part of me still can't believe that only a few days ago, she was on the back of this bike, clinging to my waist and laughing in my ear like we were the only two people in the entire world. She inhabits a moment so easily, no thought for what comes next or what's come before. Jaz Whitaker is the textbook definition of living in the present.

The light goes green, and I rev my engine. I know how to live in the moment, right? I have a motorcycle, for heaven's sake. I take off down the road, trying to outpace the thought that maybe Jaz is right, maybe I *am* missing out on something essential by keeping this place at arm's length. How can that be true when I'm literally winding through its streets, exploring Itaska's inner workings like Dad would one of his project cars?

A blaring honk startles me. "Slow down, idiot!" someone yells from a car I've just passed.

Flustered, I pull to the left of the one-way street and turn off onto a side road. I take a few random turns, hoping to calm the thoughts running through my head. I'm breathing hard, hands sweaty. Suddenly, everything feels too tight. I slide into the first parking spot I see and rip off my helmet to get some air.

When I finally get myself to settle down, I look at my surroundings. It's a part of town I've never been to, located outside the "historic main street" area where Oma and Opa live. There's an American Legion building across the street with a parking lot occupied only by potholes. A gas station on the corner is plastered in posters for things like the high school play and a battle of the bands at a local bar. I've pulled over next to a rundown place called Best of Three Sports & Games. Its front display is a tableau of a baseball umpire uniform and a figure skating leotard made to look like they're sitting at a table with a half-finished 1000-piece Baby Yoda puzzle.

I pat my pocket before remembering I left my phone on the couch. I don't recognize any of the street names, and I genuinely don't think I can retrace my steps to find my way home. I wasn't thoughtfully taking turns. I was just driving.

Curse you, living in the moment!

I climb off my bike and walk to the end of the block, looking up and down the road for any landmarks I recognize. Nothing. I go back and check the other cross-street. I know I came from the right, but that's about it. The rest is a mystery to me.

I kick a landscaping rock that's escaped from a flower bed along the sidewalk. Guess I'll have to swallow my pride and ask for directions. Ugh.

Before I turn to try the Sports & Games store, my gaze snags on a familiar ponytail bouncing behind a row of parked cars.

"Jaz!"

She's across the bigger street, jogging away from me. A set of white earbuds tells me she didn't hear my yell. I wait for a break in traffic and sprint across the road.

"Hey Jaz, wait up!"

God, this girl's fast. I get to the sidewalk and take off after her. Even pumping my legs as fast as they can move, I barely manage to catch up. She looks like she's jogging at a leisurely pace, the monster. I tap her shoulder and then stop running, hands on my knees.

"Kendall? What are you doing here?"

By the time I look up, she's stopped on the sidewalk, earbuds in her hands. She's not even breathing heavily. I'm fighting for my life over here.

"Got lost . . . on my bike." I can hardly get the words out. "Saw you . . . running."

Her eyes light up. "Ooh, are you coming to beg for help? Love that for me. Where'd you park?"

I try to convince her to show me directions on her phone, but Jaz insists on getting taken for a ride again. When she asks where I need to go, I hesitate.

"Uh, I was heading for Schultz Music. You know, that store on—"

"I know it! That place is the best."

It turns out I wasn't even that far from home. Jaz directs me by squeezing my arm and pointing whenever we should turn, and the ride only takes a few minutes. I'm honestly embarrassed I couldn't figure it out on my own.

"Thanks," I say sheepishly after I cut the engine in front of the shop. "Do you want me to take you somewhere? I feel bad for interrupting your run."

"I was almost done anyway."

"*That's* what almost done looks like for you? Do you even *have* sweat glands?"

She giggles. "I paced myself. Besides, I've been needing to pick up a new drum key. I'll come in with you."

Instant panic. If I go in with Jaz, Oma will absolutely say hi, reveal she's my grandmother, and ask tons of questions about the girl I've brought "home." If I change my mind about visiting the shop, Jaz is going to be hurt, confused, and/or pissed off. There's no way I'm getting out of this unscathed.

I follow Jaz inside, feeling like a death row inmate being led to her doom. The bell above the door jingles, but I duck behind a display before I can be spotted.

"Evening."

It's Opa's voice. Jaz greets him back, shooting me a weird look.

"I'm just looking at these, uh . . ." I pick the first thing I see. ". . . Kazoos."

If Opa's working the register, Oma is probably taking her break up in the apartment. I chance it and emerge from my hiding spot.

"Oh hi, *sir*." I give Opa my most meaningful, please-read-my-mind-and-don't-acknowledge-you-know-me look. "Sorry we're in right before closing."

Opa's eyebrow hairs are so long and thick they cast shadows over his eyes. His expression is hard to read. "Not a problem. Let me know if you need anything."

And then he leaves us to ourselves. Bless that man and his introversion.

"What are you looking for?" Jaz asks me as we browse the aisles.

I think quickly, coming up with something I know we don't carry. "I was going to see if they have synthetic reeds." Oma doesn't believe in such heresy.

As predicted, we find none of those and plenty of drum keys for Jaz to choose from. She makes her choice and checks out with Opa at the register. I lurk by the guitar amps.

I'm starting to think we'll make it without incident when the side door that leads to the hallway opens.

"Why, *hello*, Kendall!" She sounds surprised but glad, though I'm not sure whether it's from seeing me in the shop before closing or seeing me with a kid from school. Probably both.

"We were just heading out." I grab Jaz's arm and drag her out the door with me. "Good to see you, Angelika!"

I hear Oma's confused voice begin, "Did she just—" before the door swings shut and I'm safe on the sidewalk with Jaz.

"Nice, I didn't know you'd met Angelika Schultz! She's a wizard. Love that lady."

"Yeah, she's sure something!" I tug her toward my

bike. "Here, let me give you a ride home."

***

"ARE YOU POSITIVE you have everything?"

"Yes, Dad."

"Black socks? Sweatshirt? That little flip folder for your pep band music?"

"Yes, yes, and yes," I say. "We're playing our first football game, not shipping out to Baghdad. I've done this before, Dad."

"I know." He runs a hand through his beard. For the first time, I notice the brown hair has flecks of gray. "I just want it to go well for you."

"Maybe if you'd let us come watch, we wouldn't have to worry about you." Oma fusses with my backpack zippers. She's a little salty that I've banned them from coming to performances.

"Why are you guys so worked up about this? It's football. This is our *least* important type of show."

"You've just been having such a good time lately," Dad says. "Jumping in rivers, bringing a girl home . . . ."

"I did *not* bring her home. And Opa, I'm mad at you for snitching."

My grandfather's chilling in his recliner. He innocently shrugs as if he didn't betray me by telling Oma and Dad that I was with Jaz in the store. I stick out my tongue.

"In any case." Dad seems determined to keep the peace. "I want you to keep going out and having fun like that. This is the first game of the season! I remember at *our* home opener—"

"Boooo, no one wants to hear about your high school glory days." I push his shoulder playfully to let him know I'm kidding. Dad and I used to have a jokey relationship, but ever since the divorce, I feel like I need to treat him a little more gently to make up for the way Mom treated him.

"Just saying, magical things can happen when the stadium lights are on and the smell of hot dogs is in the air."

"I don't think the words 'magical' and 'hot dog' belong in the same sentence." I hike up my bag and zip my hoodie. "I think I've got everything. Will you let me go now?"

"Okay, okay." Dad pulls me into a hug. "Have a great night, kiddo."

I roll my eyes. "Thanks, Dad. See you guys later."

I squint and give Opa the two-fingered "I've got my eyes on you" gesture on my way out. He only grins back.

At school, the energy in the band room is palpable as we get into our uniforms for the first time. The band parents have spent the week hemming and adjusting, making sure everything's perfect for our first performance in full dress. I'm in a pair of black biker shorts and a black tank top. I slide on the deep blue pants with suspender straps that will be hidden by my jacket. Madison's brought a Bluetooth speaker, and half the band is belting along with "Bohemian Rhapsody." Jaz is in the Cave, already dressed, drumming on a practice pad balanced atop Emilio's head. Gavin is going over time signature changes in a corner. Michael leans against the wall next to Miss Alvarez, saying something that makes her burst out laughing—no small feat.

I've been in three different bands in high school, and the time before a performance is the same everywhere. The chaos, the nerves, the B.O. What's new here is the fizzle of excitement in my stomach.

Despite what I said to Dad, I'm looking forward to being out there on the field with my band. Even if it is just a football game.

I'm about to slip on my jacket when I realize I need to pee.

"I'll be right back," I tell Madison. "Don't let them head out without me."

"Are you going to the bathroom? Our normal ones are in the closed-off side of the building. You'll have to go to the basement of the fieldhouse. Want me to show you?"

I shake my head. "I can find them."

CHAPTER TWELVE

SPOILER ALERT: I can't find them. Five minutes later I'm still wandering the labyrinthine passages of the fieldhouse basement. I pass an empty weight training room, multiple locker rooms—locked, of course—and a space with a massage bed and an ice bath. Nice. Wish we had that.

But no bathrooms.

I turn a corner to a jump scare—the two Itaska High mascots, hawk and velociraptor. They're only wearing the body parts of their costumes, animal heads abandoned on the ground, and their tongues are 100% in each other's mouths.

I clap a hand over my own mouth so I don't gasp at the sight of my new school's two weird mascots hooking up in a basement hallway. They're so wrapped around each other I can barely make out distinct features on either. I *think* it's a guy with long, brown hair and a girl with short, blond hair. Or is it the opposite? I duck back behind the corner and press my back against the wall, wheezing with silent laughter.

My first thought is how I can't wait to tell Jaz about this. My second thought is to berate myself for the first. Have I let myself get to the point where I want to share everything funny that happens with her? I roll my eyes and peek around the wall. The mascots are still going at it, and I notice now that the sign for a bathroom is directly above them. Because of course it is.

Only way out is through, I tell myself. *Be brave.*

My anxiety is unfounded. The two raptors are so wrapped up in each other that I'm basically invisible as I sneak around them and into the bathroom. I pee and hustle back to the band room, where Miss Alvarez is leading everyone through a quick warm-up. Even if I wanted to tell Jaz anything, the battery is already outside doing its own thing in the lot next to the dumpster. I can hear the tap-tap-tap of their drills through the exterior door, which has been wedged open with a marimba mallet.

After warm-ups, Michael leads us outside to march, four people wide, with Gavin at the front and the drumline at the back.

"Remember, folks, this is your first public performance of the show music!" Michael keeps up by shuffling sideways, like the drills Jackson does at basketball practice. "I want to see that pride in your eyes. Show 'em what the Itaska Marching Band is about!"

We arrive at our football field and file in through a gate behind the bleachers. Itaska's team, decked out in navy blue jerseys and gold helmets, is huddled near our sideline with some coaches. The opposing team is warming up in white jerseys on the other side of the field. The stands are speckled with attendees. The band has a reserved section at the far end. I end up between Adam and Madison, right in front of the freshman trumpet players. *There go my eardrums.*

Attendees trickle in with their hands full of nachos and popcorn and little white Styrofoam cups of hot cocoa, even though it feels like a hundred degrees inside the thick wool fabric of my uniform. I try not to let myself feel claustrophobic—being in crowds has never been my favorite. Once we start playing, I'm able to relax a bit more. Gavin gets onto a stool at the bottom of the bleachers to lead us through a few songs from our cheesy repertoire: "Centerfold," "Uptown Funk," "Crazy Train." We play the school fight song as our team is introduced on the loudspeaker.

We sit back down as the game starts. Our team is laughably bad, and I have fun cheering with the saxes as we fumble the ball within the first minute. Occasionally Gavin calls us to attention when there's a big play or a timeout. Then he leads us through an enthusiastic, out-of-tune rendition of a pep band song from the little flip folder attached to the neck of my instrument. Itaska even scores a touchdown at the end of the first quarter, which warrants a much more enthusiastic play-through of our fight song.

We're running on pure goofy football energy as Alvarez leads us off the stands halfway through the second quarter. We line up behind the bleachers so we can take the field at halftime. I go over our music in my brain. We'll only play the opener and drum break, since a football crowd doesn't want to see a full eleven-minute marching band field show. Plus, we've only been learning the music for a few weeks.

I'm surprised to realize I'm thinking about all this in terms of "us." *We've* been learning, *our* football team, *our* music. Despite my efforts, this group of dorks has really grown on me. I should be more upset, since that's bad news for my bet with Jaz, but

I can't really get into it. I turn my head and find her gaze. She crosses her eyes at me, then starts the cadence for us to march onto the field.

For the first time in years, I feel like I'm somewhere I could belong.

***

THE PERFORMANCE STARTS off well but goes downhill from there. Jaz has a small duet with Emilio during the drum break. I hear her stick hit the rim near the beginning of it, then her part goes silent. Emilio keeps playing, a little more tentatively, and when their duet is finished, I keep an eye on Jaz as I move through the band's weird dance choreography. She's out of sync for the rest of the show.

By the time we're leaving the field, I swear I can hear her frustration in the way she plays our march-off cadence. Only a few people clap for us from the bleachers. The weakness of the cheers has nothing to do with her mistakes, of course—I've never played for a football crowd that cares about the band's halftime show—but it seems to emphasize the negative energy as we march off the field and back behind the stands.

Gavin calls, "At ease." The tuba players groan with relief as they set their heavy instruments on the ground—maybe a little too roughly, considering it's gravelly tarmac. I lift my sax and massage my neck, where all the weight sits, and watch Jaz.

Carina and Emilio are talking near her, but she's removed her drum and moved to sit on a concrete support beneath the bleachers. Her shako is off, and a couple of twists have come loose, obscuring her expression. I go to her, despite the voice in my head telling me to let her sort it out herself.

I lean against a metal pole that extends up from the concrete. In a low voice, I say, "You okay?"

She blows a raspberry and whacks her drumstick against the pole near us. "Sure."

As if I'd believe that. I've never seen this side of Jaz before. I kind of assumed she was invincible.

"What happened? You just sort of stopped."

She rounds on me, eyebrows arched downward. "Yeah, obviously. I don't need you to come over and shove it in my face. I messed up, okay? I screwed up the show for everyone."

There's a bite in her voice I haven't heard before. My first instinct is to bite back, but I stop myself. Is her reaction a bit much? Yes. Will it help anyone if I make a snarky retort? I highly doubt it.

I take off my hat and sit down next to her. By now, a chunk of the band has wandered off for concessions. We get a twenty-minute break before we have to go back and do pep band for the rest of the game. Carina shoots us a look that Jaz doesn't notice. I jerk my head to imply she and Emilio should follow the group. Her mouth twists, but she obeys.

I bump Jaz's shoulder with mine, like she always does to me. "You didn't screw it up for everyone."

"You wanna bet?"

I bite my lip to stop myself from chuckling at her vehemence. Even when she's angry, she's adorable.

"Yeah, you messed up. But guess who has no idea? The entire audience. Those people wouldn't know a sixteenth note from a crescendo. They just want us to play loud and get off the field quick enough for our team to come back and lose."

Her mouth twitches at that. Then her face turns sullen again. "I didn't even want this stupid solo. I tried to tell Alvarez, but she wouldn't hear it."

I'm shocked enough that I forget my resolution

not to be snarky. "Jaz Whitaker, avoiding the spotlight? I thought I knew you." She gives me a dirty look, and I put up my hands. "Sorry. I'm a dick."

"Don't I know it," she grumbles. A whistle sounds in the distance, starting the second half of the football game. Jaz gets up, rubbing her palms on the side of her uniform. "I lied to you."

I stand, too.

"I didn't quit drum major because I missed the music. Or that wasn't the only reason." She takes a deep breath and lets it out. "I quit because I wasn't perfect, and there was no way to hide that up in front of everybody. I knew I could hide better down with the band. And then I get stuck with this effing solo anyway." She goes back to whacking the pole with her drumstick.

I have a feeling I'm the first person she's told this. I reach out and catch her wrist before she can hit the pole again. Jaz looks down at my hand.

"I just . . . hate making mistakes," she continues, as if she can't stop herself. "When I do, I figure, why try after that? There's no way to recover, not really."

"Listen to yourself! That makes no sense." She tries to pull her arm back, but I hold firm. "Every single human person makes mistakes. Giving up the second you do isn't the answer. I am genuinely confused how you got to be so good at everything with that attitude."

"You think I'm good at everything?"

"*Stupid* good. It's annoying."

I let go of her wrist, but she catches my sleeve before my arm drops.

"You think I'm good at everything," she repeats, a smug grin spreading across her face.

"Okay, well, that's not the most important point I was trying to make—"

Jaz pulls me into a hug, sandwiching my sax between us. "Thanks, Kendall. For coming over and talking to me."

"Watch the reed," I mumble.

She shifts but doesn't let go. I tuck my face into her shoulder and inhale. We're in a goofy position, but I'm surprised to realize it feels comfortable with Jaz. It feels right. Her neck is warm against the side of my face, and our breathing syncs to unison. In and out, perfectly in time.

Jaz releases me, smiling bright and wide. She went from gloomy to her usual chipper self so quickly I have whiplash. Is that what hugging me does for her?

"Come on." She picks up her snare drum and harness, then starts off toward the concession stand. "We have to load up on nachos before break's over. I'm starving."

"That's the spirit." I walk close enough to her that our arms brush—on the side where my reed is *not* in danger. "If we don't feel sick by the end of the night, we're doing it wrong."

CHAPTER THIRTEEN

I SPEND SUNDAY morning sorting guitar strings with Dad in the kitchen. We're both in a quiet mood, which means I have plenty of time to relive that hug with Jaz in my mind, over and over. At some point, Dad puts down the nylon strings he's wrestling with and cocks his head.

"Something's up with you," he says. "But I can't tell if it's good or bad."

My traitorous cheeks heat, which I try to hide by getting up to fill a glass of water. "What do you mean?"

"Don't play innocent." He narrows his eyes, crow's feet appearing at the corners. "I'm your father. I was there when you were expelled from the womb. I know when something's up with my daughter."

"Ew, Dad. Never say 'expelled from the womb' again. Ouch!"

He's leaned forward and poked me with one of the strings, right in the arm. "You're avoiding the point."

Irritation radiates through me. I used to be an open book with my family. Jackson, Dad, Caylee, Mom—I didn't need to keep secrets from them. With all the change, they were the only people I knew I could trust.

We all know how that turned out.

Mom's garbage choices shouldn't translate to my keeping Jaz a secret from Dad. But the night I found Mom's texts was the moment our little bubble as a family burst. We've been slowly moving apart ever since, no longer each other's shields from the world. I hate to admit it, but I've even grown apart from Jackson and Caylee. It's hard to stay close when you live a thousand miles away. Throw in puberty, and it's nearly impossible.

Dad and I live together, but I don't have to tell him everything. I'm my own person.

"Everything's normal, okay?" I sit down at the table and flick a ragged packet of strings into the "toss" pile. "You don't have to know every single thing about what I do. I'll be an adult in a couple months. I'm not your little kid anymore."

He sighs. I don't meet his eyes.

"Okay," he says. "That's fair." He's not sorting anymore, just watching me with this look on his face, like he's got a whole mix of emotions and can't seem to pick one. "Why don't you get out of here for a bit? I can finish up. It's the weekend. Text your band friends—see what they're doing."

I leave the house, but I don't text anyone. Instead, I wander through the residential streets behind the apartment until I find a small lake. The sun has started to set, and there's a breeze in the air that hints at the upcoming fall. I watch ducks slip their heads underwater to catch fish while a squirrel chitters from a tree somewhere above. A young family with two little girls walks ahead of me on the trail. The sound of toddler laughter and the gentle lap of waves against the shore are so calming that eventually, I almost forget about the conversation with Dad and the feeling of Jaz's arms around my neck.

Almost.

***

THAT WEEK, JAZ acts the same toward me—her usual amount of flirty and friendly. Maybe I was the only one who thought our hug after the football game was A Moment. I was probably just reading into things.

So I act normal, too, pretending to still be New Kendall instead of I'm-Starting-To-Obsess-Over-You Kendall. I'm especially careful because Adam has taken to looking between the two of us when we're talking, eyes narrowed as if we're a puzzle he's trying to solve. Jaz usually smacks him when he does it and calls him creepy.

Once, Adam and I are the first ones in our section to arrive for rehearsal. He looks around, leans my way, and half-whispers, "Are you and my sister conspiring on something?"

"Pardon?" I say primly as I apply a tube of cork grease to my sax's crumbling neck cork. I should probably have Oma look at that.

"Something's up between you two. I can feel it." He frowns. "But the question is, what? Are you planning a surprise birthday party for me? Plotting my demise? So many options. . . ."

I try not to visibly sigh with relief. He doesn't know things have changed with Jaz and me. He's just a strangely observant but rather self-centered little brother. I make a mental note to ask Jaz when Adam's birthday is. I have a feeling he'd go nuts for that Baby Yoda puzzle I saw at the game store.

"You're imagining things," I say in my now-practiced New Kendall voice. "Spend more time focusing on hitting all the notes in that run in the closer. I heard you miss a natural yesterday."

"Wait, you did?" As predicted, he rifles through his music to find the offending selection. "Are you sure? Show me where it was."

***

MOM 11:05 AM
When's your Homecoming weekend?
Hello?

Kendall 11:55 AM
Mom, you gotta stop texting me during school
And idk, why do you need to know?

Mom 11:59 AM
I was thinking me and the kids could visit! It would be the perfect Time. The kids have a three-day Weekend, and I'm alumni, after all.

Kendall 11:59 AM
Mom. No.

We miss half of Friday's woodshop class for a talk in the library from college recruiters, including one from the University of Michigan. I've been planning on going there for a few years. I don't know why I'm fixated on it, but Michigan is one of the states we've never lived, a place I don't know anything about and have no connections to. Plus, they have a good engineering program. I can start new, finally be my own person. Usually daydreaming about that hazy day in the future cheers me up, but for some reason, I feel myself growing more and more irritated as the recruiter talks. It probably doesn't help that I'm on my period, and the cramps are killing me. Combine that with Mom's suggestion that she come visit—which will no doubt ruin all of Dad's progress—and I'm in a crummy mood by the time band class rolls around.

I head to the Cave without thinking about it, hopeful a glimpse of Jaz will cheer me up. The percs are throwing darts at a board with a jaguar mascot on it.

Jaz watches from the back of the room as Carina and the boys try and fail to get a bullseye. "What's that about?"

"Our show this weekend's at McKinley High. They're our sworn enemies."

"Seems healthy."

Emilio throws a dart that lodges into the wall six inches from the dart board. Something tells me this is not an Alvarez-approved activity.

"Maybe not, but McKinley's the worst. The way the boundaries work out in our district, they get all of the newer housing developments, which are mostly rich Californians coming to escape the cost of living. So all their programs are super well-funded, including the band. We're on opposite ends of the 2A division because their band is the biggest it can be and ours is one of the smallest."

"Ah, classic," I keep my eyes on the dart game, worried Emilio will hit me. "Rich school versus poor school. Tale as old as time. Pretty sure my last school was the McKinley in this situation."

Jaz turns to me. "Where *did* you go before this, anyway? You never talk about your old schools."

"Not much to talk about," I say. "I went to a bougie school in Colorado Springs last year. Freshman and sophomore year I was in Chicago. Did band all four years. Had no friends. You know, the usual."

Jaz sniffs. "At least you have friends now."

"Do I?" The words are out of my mouth before I can stop them. I realize immediately how bratty I sound, but it's too late to take it back.

Jaz arches one of her well-shaped eyebrows. "Uh, yes? At least, I thought that's what we were." She gestures to herself and the percs, to Adam and Matty in the band room. "Do you feel differently?"

I choose my words carefully. "It's just that . . . we've known each other for less than a month. Can you really be friends with someone you've known for that short of time? In my mind, a friend is someone you grew up with, someone you share everything with. You don't even know where I live."

Her eyes bug out. "Yeah, because you won't tell me! What the heck, Kendall? Everybody's welcoming you in. And you still insist on saying crap like that. I don't get you."

"Sorry my inability to love is inconvenient for you."

She rolls her eyes so hard I'm afraid they'll pop out of her head. "Whatever, Mathis. Feel free to keep living your lonely life. I guess that's what you do. And we'll keep inviting you to crap and being nice to you, because that's what *we* do."

"Sounds great."

"Cool."

"*Cool.*"

CHAPTER FOURTEEN

KENDALL 6:44 AM
Sorry about yesterday. I was in a weird mood.

I wake to the sound of an August rainstorm tinkling on my window. Opa makes waffles and scrambled eggs and iced tea for breakfast, and I stuff my face till I can hardly move. I need the energy for a long day of marching, after all. Plus, I'm eating my feelings after Jaz's only response to my apology is a thumbs up emoji. That's a lot of passive-aggression in one icon.

The weather means I'll have to cop a ride off Dad instead of taking the bike. He's still sleeping when I need to go, so I knock on his door.

"Hummph?"

"Hey, Dad," I say. "It's raining. Do you think you could drive me to the school?"

I hear him sit up, groan, and stretch.

"Yeah, I'm coming." He emerges in the shirt and jeans he wore yesterday. What little hair he has on his head sticks up in all directions. His eyes have bags underneath them.

"Didn't sleep well?"

Dad's insomnia is one of the things Mom complained about the most: his shifting in bed, staying up watching movies on his phone with headphones, pacing the kitchen. She said it was ruining *her* sleep, and she needed to be rested when she consulted with clients. She hadn't seemed concerned in the least that this was affecting Dad, too.

He nods. "Took me hours to conk out. No worries. I'll take a nap later. Unless . . ."

"I told you guys, don't come. It's boring. We're on the field for, like, ten minutes, and I guarantee we won't win anything."

"We'd be going to support you." He somehow looks even more tired as he rubs a hand over his face. "We don't care if you win."

"And it's the thought that counts! Boom. I feel supported."

When Dad drops me off at school, I sprint to the door so my instrument case doesn't get too wet. The air conditioning against my damp skin makes me shiver, and my shoes squeak against the linoleum on my way to the music room. The band room smells horrendous, like a hundred wet dogs. Everyone's a little more reserved than usual as they shake water off their backpacks and jackets.

"We'll rehearse inside today," Miss Alvarez announces with a clap of her hands. "Forecast says there's a possibility this lightens up by tonight, so we're operating under the hopes that it does. Hopefully you all worked hard on your sets yesterday while I was at my dentist appointment."

"No need to worry," Michael chimes in from where he's sitting cross-legged on the floor next to the mellophones. "I was a straight-up taskmaster. Right, kids?"

"Right!" we all lie. Michael spent half of Friday's practice waxing eloquent on the power of music education. He may have teared up at one point. Not to mention all the darts playing in the Cave.

Adam is as chatty as usual today, so I figure Jaz hasn't complained about me to him. She seems happy enough, joking with Carina and Emilio while the band does tonal warm-ups. I can't tell if she's intentionally not looking my way.

Chill out, I tell myself. *This is for the best.*

We play through our ballad, a rendition of "Come Fly with Me," to the sound of rain on the roof and low, distant thunder.

"Is that a bad sign?" I ask Adam when Alvarez stops the band to work with the low brass on their intonation.

He shrugs. "My dad always says, 'If you don't like the weather in Minnesota, just wait a few minutes!'"

"That is an extremely dad thing to say." It's also something I've heard in nearly every state we've lived in, but I don't tell him that.

For the drive to McKinley, Adam abandons me for what Madison calls the "terror bus," mostly being boarded by underclassmen and color guard. Then Madison leaves me for her sister, and Jake, the quiet tenor sax player, takes a seat next to a sophomore he has apparently started dating, despite my never having seen them speak to one another before now. Good for him, I guess.

I end up next to Matty, who's only alone because Alyssa's family wants to drive her to our closest-to-home field show. He's not a bad bus buddy, much less chatty and emotionally frustrating than Jaz.

She's three rows ahead of me, deep in conversation with Gavin, Alvarez, and Michael. I glare at the back of her head for most of the ten-minute bus ride.

The rain has stopped by the time we arrive at McKinley High, though dark clouds still linger in the distance. We unload and rehearse some more in half-uniform, leaving our jackets and shakos in the trailer until it's time to take the field. The air is the kind of wet cold that seeps past your skin and into your bones. I try to tough it out, but eventually I give up and jog to our things by the bus. I grab my favorite bomber coat from my backpack to go over my overalls and T-shirt.

"Excuse me, ma'am, this flowery thing is not regulation."

Michael's arms are occupied with boxes full of paper lunch bags, so he gestures at my jacket with his head. I freeze, like I've been caught robbing a bank.

"I'm just messing with ya, K-Dawg," he says. "How are things going, by the way? It looks like you've adjusted pretty quickly to the Itaska way of things."

News to me. I shrug. "Fine, I guess."

"That's good to hear." He leans toward me conspiratorially. "I actually moved a lot as a kid, too. Army brat. I hated it."

"You did?" I can't imagine Michael, the human embodiment of the "Hang in There!" cat, hating anything.

"Oh yeah, I was your typical tortured teenager. Skinny jeans, black hair in my face, the whole shebang. Can you imagine?" He gestures at his current self, now a lot closer to *cool youth pastor* than *emo kid.* "Anyway, my point is that there's light at the end of the tunnel. Someday you, too, can be an elementary music teacher who hangs out with smelly teens after school to supplement your disturbingly low income."

For some stupid reason, Michael's inspirational speech works on me. The weather stays overcast, but energy is high as we go from rehearsing to a lunch of sandwiches, apples, and chips served up by the parent volunteers. People keep spontaneously shouting "Show day!" followed by echoes from the rest of the band. We sound like the seagulls in *Finding Nemo*. I sit at a picnic table with Matty, Alyssa, and the other flutes and play a game that involves a lot of slapping down cards and yelling at each other. Alyssa, who's normally pretty sweet, is *brutal*. When Matty tries to cheat and slip a card under hers, she curses him out so loudly we get scolded by one of the moms.

Despite myself, my gaze wanders to where the percs are eating. But Jaz isn't there. She's off on a bench next to the baseball field, running through her solo on a practice pad. Her brows are knitted together in concentration, and when she trips up, she makes a frustrated noise and chucks her drumstick into the dirt.

"Is she always like this?" I whisper to Matty. A self-centered part of me wonders if she's acting like this because of our argument yesterday.

He follows my gaze and nods. "We've learned to just leave her alone."

But I can't. No matter what I do, I can never seem to leave Jaz alone. She's upset. What if she needs someone to talk to? Maybe she wishes they *wouldn't* keep their distance but at this point is too proud to ask. It's hard to let people in when you don't feel like you deserve it.

I excuse myself from the card game and make my way to where she sits. She picks up her stick and goes back to practicing, not making eye contact.

"You know it already, Jaz," I say gently. "You're just psyching yourself out at this point."

"I've just gotta get this one part." She drums furiously. Her arms are tense, her jaw muscle popping. There's this glimmer in her eyes, something sharp-edged and wild, that makes me push further.

"Jaz," I say. "Jaz!"

She slams her sticks down on the pad and jerks her head up. "What?!"

"You're freaking me out, woman! Are you always like this at shows?"

Jaz doesn't answer for what feels like an eternity. She stares across the field at another band's color guard working through their tosses. There are five of them, and only two are catching their rifles on any given attempt.

On the next try, every rifle hits the ground. Jaz sighs. "Sometimes. Messing up at the football game didn't help things."

I sit on the end of her bench, close enough to be comforting but far enough that our arms don't run the risk of touching. "A little intense, don't you think?"

"I just want to get it right." She deflates, shoulders slumped. "I *have* to get it right."

I'm overwhelmed by an impulse—no, a need—to comfort her. I hesitate. Since I met Jaz, the dynamic between us has been stop-and-go traffic. Late night bonding at band camp? Foot on the gas. Tell her I don't want a girlfriend? Slam on the brakes. Jump into a river with our clothes on? Pedal to the metal. It's like emotional whiplash.

Jaz is still breathing heavily, chest rising and falling beneath her black ribbed tank top. If I can just calm her down, that will be enough.

My fingers brush her sleeve. "Hey, look at me." I use the soothing but neutral voice I normally reserve for Dad when he's in a spiral. When she meets my eyes, I say, "Let me take a guess. Are you a perfectionist, by any chance?"

Despite herself, Jaz snorts a little laugh. She drops her forehead onto my shoulder. "May-be." She draws the word out, like she's not willing to fully admit it.

I move my thumb back and forth on her arm, clocking the way her breath slows and her jaw relaxes. She shifts so her right temple is on my shoulder and our hips are parallel. The rest of the band carries on twenty feet away, everyone too wrapped up in themselves to notice two girls sitting side by side, pulses syncing to a steady tempo.

"You're an incredible drummer," I say, meaning it. "I've seen what you can do. And yeah, you make mistakes sometimes. It's because you're a freaking human being. What matters is how you act *after* you make those mistakes. You've got to forgive yourself, hold your head up, keep trying. Can you do that for me?"

"How are you so mature? You're a middle-aged woman in a teenage girl's body." I feel her smile against my arm.

"Girl, you *know* I've got my own problems." I flap a hand to gesture at my entire self. "But perfectionism is not one of them. I'm content with my mediocrity, thank you very much."

"You're not mediocre," she says, more firmly than I'm expecting.

My cheeks warm at the certainty in her voice.

"Wasn't fishing for compliments."

I seem to have successfully distracted Jaz, because she lifts her head to give me a *look*. This is a new one, something mischievous and heavy-lidded and liquid.

"You sure? Don't want me to convince you?"

My soul straight-up leaves my body. She tips forward, face so close alarm bells start going off in my head: *Alert! Pretty girl's mouth is inches away!*

"I—uh—" My brain can't form sentences anymore. *Code red!*

A shrill whistle splits the air. We jump apart, awkwardly giggling, flustered.

"We should get going." Jaz's voice is a half-octave higher than before.

My mind is in crisis mode. What was I thinking? I'd gotten so caught up in her closeness, in the emotions, in her adamance that I was worth sticking up for. She'd been leaning toward me, right? My mind flashes through what might have happened if Gavin's whistle hadn't ruined the moment, a rapid-fire montage of images that makes my neck heat up. *Why do we keep getting interrupted?*

I have no idea what to say or what to do. So I choke out, "Sorry," jump to my feet, and sprint toward the rest of the band.

CHAPTER FIFTEEN

JAZ KILLS HER duet with Emilio at the show. Their rhythm and musicality are on point, and neither makes a single mistake. I feel like cheering when they finish their final run, but I have to snap my horn up because the whole band starts the closer with a crescendo into a loud, brassy company front.

After the show, Gavin leads us off the field to Jaz's cadence. We wind away from the stands, around the corner of the school, until we reach our spot next to our trailer. The second Gavin calls "at ease," someone in the trombone section whoops. A few others cheer, and I'm given high fives by at least four people.

"That. Was. *Fantastic!*" Michael shouts once we settle down. "You all should be very proud of what you did out there. We'll have to wait and see what the judges think, but I *know* that you left it all out on the field. And that's all we can ask for, really."

"I just had a few critiques," Alvarez says, pulling out a notebook. "Let's see, what did I write? Oh yeah, nothing, because I was too blown away the whole time."

Now everyone really does cheer. Alvarez never praises us like this. In the chaos, I end up near Jaz.

I work up the courage to speak. "Nice job. Knew you could do it."

She lowers her lashes. "Thanks."

"Oi!" Carina calls from a huddle of percussionists. "Come get naked!"

Jaz laughs at my bewildered expression and walks backward, away from me. "Gotta change out of uniform together. It's tradition!"

I scoff. Another weird rule. I'm getting used to it, though. The traditions are starting to be comforting instead of strange. Like I'm starting to understand why they have them all in the first place.

***

I PULL INTO the parking lot a few minutes past midnight, still running on a high from the near-kiss with Jaz and a successful first field show. We took second only to McKinley. Back in Colorado, Evelyn High's band was accustomed to being dominant, which made competitions kind of boring. And during my two years in Rockford, Illinois, our band came in last in the division almost every time. I can live with runner-up. Jaz wasn't pleased, but she also wasn't surprised. We always get second to McKinley.

I unlock the door and drop my bags and instrument case, then rest against the wall for a moment, reliving the night. When I come back to Earth, I realize the TV's on in the living room.

I walk around the corner to find Dad on the couch, wrapped in a blanket with his legs on the coffee table. There's a sandwich on the table made with peanut butter and something that looks suspiciously like marshmallow creme. The TV blares with some kind of cooking competition show.

Dad sees me and reaches for the remote, pausing his show. "Hey, sweetie. Welcome home."

"Thanks." I peer at the screen, where a woman in a pink top hat is trying to put out a fire on a stove. "What are you watching?"

"The Great American Grilled Cheese Showdown," he says a little sheepishly. "It's kind of riveting."

"Did you get inspired?" I gesture at the sandwich.

"We were out of cheese, so I worked with what I had."

"I thought you were gonna get to sleep early today." I feel like a mom even saying it. "What happened? Are you spiraling?"

He exhales heavily and brings his feet down from the coffee table, wiping a big hand over his face. "Something like that."

I drop down on the couch next to him. "Talk to me."

"It wasn't anything specific this time," he says wearily. "Got to thinking about how much I've failed you and Jackson and Caylee. I was supposed to work on the Henrys' car tonight, but I didn't, and that made me feel guilty, and eventually I just ended up watching . . . this." He gestures at the literal fire on-screen. "I can't seem to force myself to get ready for bed."

"Well, are you at least enjoying the show?"

"Not really." He chuckles humorlessly. "These people are insane. The dude in the back served the judges a sandwich made with Velveeta and canned peaches. It was horrendous."

"That *does* sound pretty bad." I snag the remote and hit the power button. "Come on. It's late. I'm tired. You look tired. Let's both get ready for bed."

He stands with a grunt, dusts some crumbs off his shirt, and shoots me an affectionate look. "How are you so responsible? Your two parents are in the dictionary under the words 'hot mess.' What did we do to deserve you?"

I'm reminded of what Jaz said about me being a middle-aged woman in a teenage girl's body. For some reason, it's a lot more irritating coming from Dad. I'm glad he's acknowledging what he and Mom put me through. I've tried hard to be a steadying force for the family during a time when it feels like one extra push might send us all crumbling to the ground. But sometimes *I* want be the hot mess. Ordinary teenagers talk back to their parents and sneak out at midnight and fall in love and get busted by the cops at parties. I ride a motorcycle, sure, but with loads of safety precautions. I feel like I'm already an adult, but I'm just now realizing that's not quite what I want.

CHAPTER SIXTEEN

ADAM WHITAKER 8:59 AM
   T-4 hours!

Adam Whitaker 10:00 AM
   T-3 hours!!

Adam Whitaker 11:11 AM
   2 hours to go! Get hype Kendall!!!!!!

I wake to the chime of the third text. I must have been sleeping so deeply the first two didn't even register. I usually put my phone on silent at night, but I was so exhausted yesterday I passed out the second my head hit my pillow. I didn't even plug into the charger.

At some point this past week, I'd idly agreed to Adam's invitation to come work on his latest puzzle Sunday afternoon. Had I completely forgotten about that commitment? Yes, yes I had. I shoot him a thumbs up emoji and lie back against my pillow, groaning. What have I gotten myself into?

There's a note in the kitchen written in Oma's

square handwriting: *We're at movie matinee. Didn't want to wake you. Apple pancakes in fridge.*

After a brunch of toaster pancakes and a long, hot shower, I find my way to the address Adam sent me. It's less than ten minutes away, deep into a neighborhood with winding roads and sweeping green lawns. The houses are big but look lived in: covered RVs in driveways, kids' bikes on porches, overturned canoes in the backyard. I ride past a family getting out of a minivan in church clothes. One of the little boys points at my bike and screams, though I can't tell if it's out of fear or excitement.

I double check my phone once I arrive to make sure I have the right house number. The Whitaker home is at the end of a long driveway, dwarfed by sugar maples that look like they've been around since Minnesota became a state. A set of stairs lead down toward a river barely visible through the thick foliage.

I park at the top of the driveway, out of the path of both garage doors. The house is made of brick and wood in tasteful dark colors, and neatly landscaped flower beds guide me to the front porch. I don't even have a chance to ring the doorbell before the door swings open to reveal Adam in sweatpants and a Captain America T-shirt, his eyes bright with excitement. "You came!"

"Uh, yeah, duh, I said I would." I step inside and rub his head affectionately. The house is cozier and more cluttered than I expected from the large exterior. A baby grand piano takes up most of the sitting room, sheet music stacked on its lid. A basket of unfolded laundry waits to be brought down a set of carpeted stairs. "Now where's that puzzle you've been telling me about?"

"I may have already gotten started," he admits as he leads me into the basement, where a large card table is covered in puzzle pieces. The rectangular frame of an autumnal landscape has already been assembled. "I couldn't help myself."

I gasp in mock astonishment.

"Do you want a tour before we start?" he offers. "I can show you around."

"Sure."

He leads me around the basement first. There's a foosball table next to the card table, and across the room is a cushy sectional couch in front of a projector screen. Every flat surface is covered in knick-knacks and family photos. On a shelf mostly full of antique model cars, a kindergarten-aged Jaz beams out from a popsicle stick frame, her front tooth missing. Adam shows me his room, where the floor is covered in dirty clothes and books and board games. The curtains are made from a Jolly Roger pirate flag.

"I was supposed to clean up before you came," Adam says. "Oops."

Outside his room is another door, which he flings open without knocking.

Jaz is propped on her stomach, chin in hands, on top of a deep violet bedspread. A tablet is propped in front of her, and she's chatting with someone on the screen.

"—haven't gotten anything done all day, even though I'm supposed to be working on that essay. I keep thinking about—"

Her head shoots up at our intrusion and she cuts off her sentence. She stares from Adam to me with wide, startled eyes.

A familiar voice on the tablet says, "Jaz? You

there?"

I lift my fingers in a weak wave. "Uh, hi. I'm guessing Adam didn't tell you I'm hanging out with him today?"

Her eyes narrow as she turns her gaze on her brother. "No, Adam did not," she says with venom, then turns back to me. "I was just . . . talking to Carina. Say hi, Carina," she says weakly.

"Speak of the devil." Carina's little pixelated face still manages to give me the feeling that I'm being evaluated—and not passing the test. "Hey, Kendall."

"This is Jasmine's room," Adam says, oblivious to the awkwardness. "It always smells like gym shorts."

Jaz scoffs and chucks a notebook at him from the pile on her bed. "It does not!"

Adam easily dodges the projectile, cackling. He doesn't expect the second one, though, and it hits him square in the chest.

"Oof!"

"Serves you right, twerp."

"I was just gonna do a puzzle with Adam," I say as I back out of the room. "He wanted to show me around. We'll . . . leave you alone."

I drag Adam with me and shut the door. "I thought you said she was out!" I whisper-yell. "She was obviously not expecting to see me."

"Whoops." He doesn't look ashamed at all.

"Great." I roll my eyes as we move back down the hallway. Adam sits at the folding table, apparently forgetting about the rest of our tour. "She seemed kind of pissed."

"She'll be fine." Adam sorts through the pieces until he finds a green one that looks identical to twenty others, and he presses it into a spot near the bottom of the puzzle. "Trust me, she's not mad at *you*. Pretty sure that's literally impossible. Did you guys kiss or something?"

I just about choke on my own tongue. "Why—did you see—?" I can't stop my cheeks from heating up. "What makes you say that?" I finally get out.

"Jaz has been sooo annoying all day, lying around and smiling to herself and sighing. Plus she keeps calling Carina with the door shut."

So much for keeping things secret from Adam. "Well, we did *not* kiss. Just so you know."

He shrugs. "Okay. She's totally obsessed with you, just so *you* know. I legit caught her doodling your name in one of those notebooks the other day."

My heart leaps, then it immediately takes a nose dive. Jaz is *into* me. Like, mooning around the house levels of into me. I never in a million years thought a girl like her would be doodling my name. I feel hot all over, my body itchy and tingling. I can't seem to focus on the puzzle. The pieces could be Cheez-Its for all the progress I'm making.

This is exactly what I was trying to avoid in the first place, the reason I tried to get Jaz to stay away from me. I need to take care of Dad. I need to graduate and go to college in Michigan and get into the engineering program. I can't have a girlfriend, especially not one like Jaz. She puts her whole heart into whatever she does. If Jaz were my girlfriend, she wouldn't half-ass it. She's the best at everything, and I have no doubt she would be an incredibly loyal, attentive, fun, perfect girlfriend.

And what would I be in return? Distant. Distracted. Always trying to find ways to avoid the next step, trying to find ways to let her down gently.

Jaz doesn't deserve that. She deserves someone

who'll make her their whole life, who'll treat her like a queen. That person isn't me.

Claustrophobia bubbles up in my chest. I have to get out of this basement *now*. I pull out my phone and pretend to read a text.

"Oh shoot, I have to get going. My dad needs me to help him with . . . something," I finish pathetically.

Adam looks at me from beneath his brows, skeptical. "Okay . . ."

"I'm really sorry," I say. "I wish I could stay longer. Text me a pic of your progress today, 'kay?" I gather my stuff and escape up the stairs.

***

I ARRIVE AT school Monday with a newfound determination. I'm going to put Jaz in the friend zone.

Sure, I started this year not even planning to make friends. But I'm full-on freaked out by my accidental glimpse into Jaz's feelings yesterday. She may have weaseled her way into my good graces, but I have to draw the line where I can—for her own good. And that line is an emphatic stroke beneath the words "JUST FRIENDS! SERIOUSLY!!"

The first time we run into each other is at lunch. Jaz grabs a fry from my tray the second I sit down.

"Thief!" I accuse. It's already halfway to her mouth.

"I can give it back." She holds the fry out with her fingers, like she's about to feed me. Her eyes sparkle.

I grab her wrist and direct the fry back toward her mouth. "Too late. It's yours."

She pouts and takes a bite. "Doesn't taste as good when I've been given permission."

"Oo, fries!" Matty snags three and shoves them in

his mouth before he's even sat down. "They must have run out before I got there."

"Want some, Carina?" She's had her nose buried in a biology textbook since I got here, hair falling into her face. She's added a streak of green to her usual black. "Everyone else is helping themselves."

"I'm good."

I've had zero luck figuring out Jaz's moody BFF. She's not outright mean to me, but if I have to shove Jaz into the friend zone to keep her at a distance, Carina feels like someone I would have to drag kicking and screaming.

If I cared about making more friends, that is.

"We don't have a show this weekend," Jaz says when she finds me after fifth period, fingers drumming on the top of the chest-height bank of lockers. "Mom's taking us to some harvest festival in a church parking lot Saturday. Want to come and overdose on caramel apples with me?"

The image of Jaz and me walking through a corn maze, dressed in flannel and UGG boots, rises unbidden in my mind. The two hands not clasped between us are holding the sticks of green apples coated in caramel so sticky we're having trouble eating them without breaking our teeth. We collapse in a fit of giggles onto a perfectly convenient set of hay bales. It's so picturesque we snap a selfie, my lips on her cheek.

"I have something with my dad that day," I lie. Enjoying adorable Itaska together might be too much, but I can at least offer an olive branch. "Adam wants me to come again to work on his puzzle this Sunday, though. I'll Venmo you if you save me an apple."

***

SINCE I'VE DECIDED to place Jaz in the friend zone, I find I'm more willing to allow Itaska as a whole into that position as well. After all, our bet was that I wouldn't fall in *love* with Itaska. I'm in no danger of that. But it wouldn't hurt to actually learn my way around my school, for one thing. The nice lady in the front office gave me a map on my first day that I promptly shoved to the bottom of my locker. Now, I'm forced to fish it out because my woodshop teacher has sent me on a mission. I'm supposed to pick up some donated driftwood from the Outdoor Adventures classroom, but I realize too late I have no idea where that is.

Map in hand, I navigate to the west end of school and receive a canvas bag filled to the brim with sticks and logs from a young, peppy teacher in a North Face pullover. I'm already on my way back when the girl I sit next to, Sarah, jogs toward me.

"Ms. Reddy sent me to show you where to go," she says, a little out of breath. She has a thin build, the kind that comes from genetics rather than a fitness obsession. "Looks like you figured it out."

"I could use some help. This thing's heavy."

She takes one handle from me, and we lug the loaded bag between us toward the classroom. Sarah's in a chatty mood, which for her means a brief minute of small talk before falling silent again. It's like we're in an introverting competition. I glance her way, trying to think of something to say. I've noticed she has a unique fashion sense, all ruffled shirts and oversized glasses. She looks a little like a character from a show I like. However, I'm pretty sure blurting "Hey, you look like that dead girl from the first season of *Stranger Things*" isn't the best way to break a silence, so I keep my mouth shut.

I'm still thinking about this when marching band rolls around. Sure, I don't need friends, but it would be nice to at least be able to hold a conversation. Sarah seems like she might be interesting, deep down inside. But we're both so socially inept that woodshop is starting to get awkward.

"How do you always have something to say?" I ask Adam during rehearsal. "Genuine question. I feel like in half of my conversations, I'm spending my brainpower trying to find a way to escape."

"I dunno. I just like people. It's one of those things that can't be taught." He whips out the opening lick of "Careless Whisper" and walks away.

I throw up my hands. "Thanks a ton."

CHAPTER SEVENTEEN

I SPEND OUR second football game squinting across the field at the Away stands.

We're playing a team from a small, rural school halfway across the state, so there are probably a dozen fans total. I'm focused on a group in the top row. The three shapes are fuzzy enough I'm starting to wonder if I should ask Sarah where she gets those oversized glasses. I'm eighty percent sure it's a woman and two men, and I'm fifty percent convinced they're Oma, Opa, and Dad. That would make no sense, though, since they'd be sitting on the Itaska side if I hadn't banned them from coming to my performances. The blurry woman and one of the men are tiny, dwarfed by the other guy, who's wearing a hunter green beanie that looks exactly like the one I got Dad for his birthday last year.

Oh god, it *is* them. Those stinkers.

I return home right as they're climbing out of the station wagon. Cutting the engine, I scold, "I'm pretty sure I made my feelings on this clear."

Opa and Dad have the decency to hang their heads, looking sheepish. Oma, however, has no shame.

"I did not immigrate to the land of the free to get bossed around by a teenager." She toddles past me with a finger waved in my face. "We wanted to see a football game. So what? Will you throw us in prison?"

I catch up to hold the door for the little traitor. "You wanted to see a game from the other team's stands?"

"We wanted to have a good view of the pep band," Dad admits. "And maybe we thought we'd be far enough to be incognito. Apparently not." He takes my sax from me and lets me through the door before following. "Don't be upset, Kendall. My therapist has been telling me to get out of the house more. This was a way to do that *and* support my oldest child."

I sigh. What am I supposed to say to that?

***

ADAM IS ALREADY on to a new puzzle by Sunday, an intricate painting of the solar system that he's apparently already completed twice.

"I've run out of new ones at our house," he says as we sit down and get to work. "Mom wants to set me up with a puzzle swap, but she hasn't gotten around to it yet."

"Sorry I was no help with the one you were working on last week."

Adam only shrugs.

"I'm serious. I bailed on you, and that wasn't cool."

"It's okay. I just thought you didn't like the puzzle."

"No way!" I rap the table with my knuckle, and he finally meets my eyes. "Adam, I promise it wasn't anything to do with you or the puzzle. Things are just . . . complicated with me and your sister. Seriously. That puzzle looked cool."

He visibly cheers up. "It was pretty good. This one has twice as many pieces, though, so it will be *even* better."

I'm hard at work on the rings of Saturn when Jaz emerges from her room in a tank top and leggings. She lays a mat down in front of the couch and pulls up a yoga video on her laptop. My chair is directly facing her as she starts doing a complicated set of moves that includes lots of pushing her chest out or sticking her butt in the air.

Adam doesn't seem to notice, chattering on about All-Conference Band tryouts in a few weeks. I split my attention between our conversation, my section of the solar system, and Jaz's measured breaths as she pushes her pelvis up into a bridge pose. It is not an equal split.

I have no clue how much time passes with me desperately trying to focus on the puzzle instead of ogling Jaz. But then she pauses the video, stretches, and pulls off her goddamn shirt. She's wearing the pink sports bra from band camp.

That girl knows *exactly* what she's doing.

Face on fire, I pick up my chair and scoot around the table till I'm crammed over on Adam's side. Now there's only a foosball table and oak bookshelf in my line of sight. Much less distracting.

Adam gives me a weird look.

I shrug. "There's a glare from that side."

***

DESPITE JAZ'S ATTEMPTS to drive me to insanity, Puzzle Sundays with Adam quickly become a regular thing. Weekends start busy, with football games and field shows, but then I get to spend a long, slow afternoon at the card table in the Whitakers' basement. Adam's endlessly entertaining. He's happy to jabber about music or video games or whatever as long as I nod every once in a while. Jaz even helps with the puzzles from time to time, although she's more often lounging on the couch, throwing out snarky comments while she scrolls her phone. There is no repeat of the yoga incident, for which I am grateful. But she does seem to wear a lot of tiny shorts and tank tops on Sundays.

Five in the evening is when I usually excuse myself to go home and have dinner with Dad and the grandparents. But one Sunday, Adam's mom pokes her head in and invites me to stay.

I haven't interacted a ton with the Whitaker parents, but when I do, they're all smiles. Jim Whitaker is a tall, solid-looking dude who always wears a button-up shirt tucked into slacks, even on weekends. Lacey Whitaker is tall, too, with an easy, graceful presence and a killer Wii tennis backhand. Adam tells me she played in college.

"I'm making pizza," Mrs. Whitaker says. "It's Adam's and Jasmine's favorite. Why don't you stick around?"

"That's a super tempting offer, but I should probably be getting home."

"I talked to your dad at the football game, and he said we can keep you as long as we want. They don't have anything special planned today."

I'm surprised enough that Dad was chatting with other parents that all I can say is, "Oh! Then thanks, Mrs. Whitaker. Pizza sounds great."

"Lacey."

"Sorry, yeah. Lacey."

Jaz cuts in front of me on my way up the stairs, which means I'm face-to-face with her tiniest pair of shorts yet. I swear they keep shrinking every week.

On the landing, I shoot her a glare as Adam passes us to go to the kitchen. She actually has the nerve to wink at me.

"Winking?" I say dryly. "In this economy?"

Jaz chuckles, and I can't stop the rush of warmth that floods me every time I hear her husky laugh. Stupid physical reactions that I can't control.

Adam inspects the pizza to make sure the toppings are, in fact, all veggies and therefore safe for me. Jim pulls out my chair, and Lacey fills my glass from the pitcher of lemonade on the table. I'm worried the focus will be on me the entire meal, but the conversation quickly devolves into a spirited discussion of some football game that happened earlier today.

As soon as the last slice of pizza disappears, Jim looks around the table and says, "How about we get the hot tub turned up? It's been a while since we've used it. Would you like to, Kendall?"

His voice is deep and kind, and before I think it through, I'm nodding.

"Wait," I blurt. "I don't have anything to wear. Maybe next time."

"No worries," Jaz pipes in. "I have just the thing."

I follow her downstairs to her room, which has an attached bathroom that smells like that cherry vanilla body wash I remember from band camp. She rifles through the back of her closet while I stand there, trying to hide the fact that I'm inhaling as much of the scent as possible.

"I doubt I'm gonna fit in one of your suits. Maybe a T-shirt and shorts?"

"Of course you're not gonna fit—I have no butt. My sister Brianna, however, does. Here we go."

The bikini she offers is aqua-colored, a single stripe

of purple going through the top and the bottom—peak 90s aesthetic.

"She left a bunch of her suits for me, but they never fit. This one kinda reminds me of you."

I can't tell if Jaz knows the pattern looks nearly identical to the bomber jacket I had on when we almost kissed at McKinley. Did she subconsciously internalize what I was wearing that day? God, that's cute.

I go into her bathroom to change. The top is tight, but Jaz was right about her sister having a butt like mine. And it really is my style.

I knock on the inside of the door. "You dressed?"

"Yep!"

I emerge from the bathroom to find Jaz posing in a bright white bikini, a dazzling contrast with her dark brown skin. The strapless top is twisted in a way that shows her cleavage, and the bottoms have high cutouts along the sides of her legs.

I turn around and shut myself back in the bathroom. "Nope!"

Jaz crows with laughter. There's a *thunk,* probably as she rests her forehead against the door, and she speaks through the wood. "What?"

"Oh, you *know* what," I grouse. "This is unfair."

"What's unfair?"

"You! You're gorgeous."

She's quiet on the other side of the door. Then, in a shy voice infused with her smile, she says, "Thanks."

In the mirror, my chest, neck, and face are splotched with red. I slump against the door, somehow exhausted and wired at the same time.

"I'm serious. I don't know if I can handle looking at you in *that* while I'm around your family. Not about to slut shame, but . . . maybe you can go up and get in the hot tub before I come out?" I blush harder. I can't help but be honest when I'm around Jaz.

Okay, not with everything—I *did* pretend Oma was a complete stranger—but with most things.

She chuckles softly. "Okay, sure. You're ridiculous."

"Oh, don't blame me," I say wryly. "You knew *exactly* what you were doing. Is this a situation where people use the word 'minx'? This feels very minx-y to me. You minx."

Now she's really laughing, full-throated, and I lean my cheek against the door so I can feel the vibrations. After she settles, I hear shifting, and then her voice is a little farther away.

"I'll see you up there."

I groan against the door. I'm so screwed.

CHAPTER EIGHTEEN

JAZ IS SAFELY underwater by the time I reach the screened-in porch that houses their above-ground hot tub. She's twisted her hair into a bun on top of her head to keep it out of the water. The jets are on and obscuring her body, thankfully, so I'm able to be a somewhat normal human being when I join her and her family.

Lacey smiles. "There you are! Glad Jaz could find you something that worked."

"Yeah, it's a really cute suit," I say.

Everyone moves on to talking about the upcoming *Star Wars* movie, about which Adam is especially passionate. He steals the spotlight, and I'm grateful. I can just sit back, enjoying the debate between Adam and his mom, who have strong but opposing views about the extended *Star Wars* universe. Jaz and Jim chip in, but I can tell they're not the nerds of the family. When they're sitting next to each other like this, it's obvious how much Jaz looks like her dad. Both have long eyelashes and small, round ears. Jim has a dimple in his left cheek, and Jaz gets a miniature version when she laughs. Even their mannerisms are the same, down to the way they sit, elbows resting on the back of the hot tub.

After about ten minutes, the debate dies down. Jim stretches his arms over his head and yawns. He looks at his wife, and they seem to have a silent conversation involving a lot of eyebrow movement and squinting. Then Jim stretches again, tucking his hands behind his head.

"Oh man, I think it's bedtime. Lacey and I are beat," he says. "And you should probably get to sleep, Adam. Don't you have quartet practice early in the morning or something?"

"No, honors quartet is Tuesday mornings, you know th—"

"In *any* case, it's time to get ready for bed. You're a growing boy. Need lots of rest."

I start to stand, too, but he waves a hand at me. "No need to be done on our account. We got the hot tub all heated up and everything. You and Jaz enjoy it a bit longer."

He sloshes to the stairs and climbs out, grabs three towels slung over a chair by the door, and distributes them to Lacey and Adam. He wraps Lacey's towel around her shoulders and gives her a hug from behind, squeezing her until she complains. Jim's arm is around her as they walk out after Adam.

The door shuts, and we're alone.

"Your parents are adorable," I say. Jaz and I are on opposite ends of the hot tub, and I have to raise my voice to be heard over the jets.

Jaz scoffs. "More like gross."

"Ah, but aren't the two inextricably connected?"

"You're hot when you say words like *inextricably,*" she deadpans as she drifts slowly to my side of the tub.

I'm mesmerized by her movement, my

commitment to the friend zone evaporating like the steam that rises from the chlorinated water. She perches on the seat next to me. Our bodies aren't touching, but I swear I can feel the heat from her leg next to mine. Which doesn't make sense, because everything's hot in a hot tub. I take in a shaky breath.

Jaz reaches over me to the control panel, presses a button, and the noisy jets turn off. She sits back and peers at me.

"You don't have to be scared of me," she says, her voice level and calm. "I don't know why you're so freaked about what's between us, but I want you to . . . I don't know. I want you to be *for* it."

I nod, but I can't think of what to say. How do I tell her how I feel if I haven't even let myself figure it out?

"You're out to your family, right? They're cool with you liking girls?"

I nod again. "They've known for years."

"We can take it slow," she says, still in that gentle tone of voice. It reminds me of how I spoke to her on that bench at the McKinley show. Like she's trying not to spook a horse. "You can tell me to back off. What about this?" She extracts my fingers from my folded arms and interlaces them with hers. We're sitting next to each other, holding hands under the water, arms resting on the slight ridge that separates our spots in the hot tub. "Is this okay?"

"Yes."

"Cool." So gentle, so reassuring. "Can I touch your hair? I love it when you wear it down like this."

"Mm-hm," I say, suddenly unable to make actual words.

She reaches across with her right hand and lifts a

lock of my hair, running the pads of her fingers along it, feeling the texture. Then she reaches up and brushes her fingers along my scalp, guiding the hair back from my face.

"That feels nice," I admit.

"I really like your hair. It's so effortlessly windswept all the time. I guess from all that motorcycle riding."

"You're hot when you use words like *effortlessly windswept*."

She hums. "I try." Her thumb runs up and down the side of my neck. I didn't know it was possible to shiver in a hot tub. "What would you do if I sat in your lap?"

"Have a heart attack, probably."

She drops her forehead to my shoulder and laughs into my skin. I want to kiss her so bad at that moment, and not just because she looks incredible in her swimsuit. I want to kiss her because she's becoming my best friend, and I'm always thinking of things to tell her, and because I've never felt this way about anyone. She makes me want to open up and let the world in.

I must show some of that in my eyes, because when she lifts her head, her expression shifts to this intense, focused look. She bites her bottom lip, unblinking, so close I could count her eyelashes. When did my arms get around her waist? When did she press herself against my side, every inch where our skin touches sparking?

"Don't be scared of me," she whispers.

I shake my head, not sure if I'm agreeing or disagreeing. I can't stop glancing down at her mouth. We're closer now. Her nose skirts along my cheek, our breath mingling.

"I said I'd only kiss you if you won the bet," she murmurs.

"You said I could have *a* kiss. Didn't say it had to be our first."

"I have no idea what I said. Probably couldn't even tell you my own name at this point." Her hand is in my hair again. "Can we kiss already?"

My brain isn't in charge anymore. I nod before I overthink it, and then her mouth is on mine, soft, moving, gone too soon. I chase the feeling, leaning in for another kiss. Even though Jaz is keeping it slow and deliberate, I know I'm already lost. Every bit of me is honed in on this pinprick of a moment, Jaz's left knee pressed into my thigh, her arms on my shoulders. Our lips separate for a breath. My hands move around her back to feel the ridges of her spine, and her eyes flutter closed briefly.

When they open again, her calm, reassuring demeanor has changed. I see heat behind her gaze.

I want to coax it out.

I lean forward, keeping eye contact as long as possible. She meets me in the middle, sealing her lips over mine with a sigh. I'm lost in her, smooth skin everywhere, soft lips, teeth, tongue. I stroke my thumbs along her ribcage and explore her mouth, taking breaks only to plant kisses along her jaw and beneath her ear. I'm gratified to hear her breath coming fast now, glad I'm not the only one losing my mind at the feeling of being together like this.

"Jaz," I whisper as she returns the favor, trailing her lips along my neck. "Jasmine. I feel like I should be calling you Jasmine right now. It's a very romantic name."

"Shut up." She nips at the spot where my neck and shoulder meet. "You think too much."

"Right."

I accept her reprimand and let myself focus again on her mouth, falling into the rhythm of her kisses, sometimes pushing and other times yielding. Heart in my throat, I smooth my hands down her lower back and skim my fingers along the hem of her swimsuit bottom. She responds by kissing me harder, molding her body to mine, and the utter abandonment in her movements makes me positive this is it, I'm going to fall for this girl, and there's nothing I can do about it.

For once, I let myself fall.

I lose track of time, lose track of where I am. I only know there's steam rising around us and Jaz's body is soft and her lips are perfect and everywhere. Our arms are so tight around each other, but it's not enough. Nothing is enough. I tug at her leg, and she straddles me in one swift moment, as if she'd been waiting for my cue. My brain short-circuits.

She registers my panic and leans back, searching my face. "You okay?"

I'm breathing like I just ran one of the sprints Jaz is so good at. I lift my hands from her thighs and lean my head back on the lip of the hot tub.

"Just . . . going a little fast."

She starts to get off me, but I clamp my hands back down on her legs to keep her there.

"No, stay. It's okay. I got overwhelmed. So much stuff was happening—*good,* good stuff—and I freaked out. I've . . . never . . . you know," I finish weakly.

"Neither have I, actually," she says, fiddling with a wet piece of my hair.

"Really?" I assumed she was more . . . free-spirited than me in that regard. She's always so comfortable with her body.

"I mean, I've gone pretty far," she says. "With

someone junior year, after I broke up with my steady girlfriend. Emma was really low-key—we didn't even kiss a lot when we were dating, and I think I kind of rebounded with the other girl." She shrugs. "We made out a lot for like a week, and then we never hung out again. I honestly wasn't that broken up about it, because I wasn't really into her. Not like I am with—"

She stops herself, but it's obvious what she was going to say. Something twists in my stomach, like my body's trying to send a message: "Warning! Dangerous waters ahead. Turn around while you still can!" *Not like I am with you.* Jaz is so earnest, so genuine with her feelings. How did I let myself get carried away? I don't want to hurt her, but there's no way I can be the kind of girlfriend she wants.

Jaz studies my face, biting her lip, then seems to make a decision. She slides away until she's floating in the center of the hot tub, no longer touching any part of me. I ache to pull her back, but I'm glad at least one of us has some self-control. I am a useless, hormone-driven need machine.

Jaz's face brightens into a smile. "I had a really nice time today. And don't worry—nothing has to change between us at school. We can just do our thing, you know? Keep it only for us."

The twist in my stomach loosens. I lean forward and plant another kiss lightly on her lips. Only one, though.

"Keeping it for us sounds perfect."

CHAPTER NINETEEN

I'M PREPARED FOR some kind of change when we return to school that week, something that reflects the seismic shift my entire being has undergone since kissing Jaz Whitaker, but she holds true to her promise. On the outside, everything is the same as it's always been. We hang out in the Cave, steal each other's fries at lunch, make fun of the clarinet section, gossip about band drama. We don't mention whatever's happening between us, and no one seems to notice. Not even Adam, although Jaz insists on telling Carina because she'll "literally perish" if she has to keep our first kiss a secret from her best friend. To Carina's credit, her behavior toward me remains as usual: a little cold, a little snarky, with just a faint hint of murderousness to keep me up at night.

In fact, the only big difference is that Jaz and I start texting every night. We talk about nothing—what we ate for dinner, what TV show we're watching, which class's homework is kicking our butts (English for me, chemistry for Jaz). There's no discussion of feelings or kissing or family drama. It's everyday stuff, stuff I usually kept to myself because I didn't think anyone cared to hear it. But Jaz does.

Dad, Oma, and Opa keep coming to our football games and field shows. They always sit in the top row on the visitor side, waving like lunatics as we march onto the field and get into our opening set. I can't wave back, obviously, but I get a stupid little glow in my heart whenever I see them there. Dad raves about me on our video calls with Jackson and Caylee, and I blush and beg him to stop. In typical Dad fashion, he doesn't.

Then there are Sundays at the Whitakers'.

It's a routine now, on its way to becoming—dare I say it?—tradition. I go to their house, do puzzles with Adam, have dinner, sometimes watch a football game or a movie with the family. Then Jaz and I sneak off to the hot tub or their dock on the river or her room to make out. Her parents are astoundingly chill about the whole thing, probably because teen pregnancy in lesbians is kind of a non-issue. We never go that far, anyway. Heart attack prevention and all that.

Life glides along like I'm in a hot air balloon, just high enough to brush my hand against the clouds. The band keeps scoring well, Dad's mental health hasn't been this good in years, and I get to be with Jaz, no relationship definition needed. I begin to wonder if I've been wrong all along, keeping a life like this at bay. What did I miss in Illinois, in Texas, in Colorado? How many experiences did I forgo, bitter in advance that I'd eventually be forced to veer off in a new direction? I could have had friends and memories spread across an entire country.

Instead I have Itaska, but it feels more like a championship run than a consolation prize.

***

THE FIELD SHOW in Marshall, Minnesota, is our

only overnighter of the season. Guess starting a four-hour drive home with two buses full of teenagers at midnight didn't seem like a safe idea to whoever plans these things. For days leading up to it, there's a buzz of anticipation at the idea of a sleepover trip now that everyone's so much closer than we were at band camp. The general vibe I've picked up is that the Marshall trip is when everything pops off with relationships in the band.

"We all thought Madison and Gavin hated each other," Alyssa informs me during a woodwind sectional. "Then Marshall comes and boom! They're inseparable."

"Chase and Arianna too, remember?" Madison protests. "We walked in on them having a DTR while *we* were looking for a place to have a DTR."

"Is DTR drugs?" Adam pipes in. "I'm gonna assume it's drugs unless you tell me."

"'Define The Relationship.'" Madison pops the gum she has somehow been chewing while playing her bari. "Pretty sure someone got pregnant on the Marshall trip, like, ten years ago. My brother told me."

"Your brother got fired from Quiznos for lying on his application," Alyssa says. "I'd take his stories with a grain of salt."

Even with romance in the air, I'm determined not to give away that Jaz and I are already . . . what? Friends with benefits? Secret smooching buddies? The past few weeks have been incredible, and I'm determined not to rock the boat.

We get an early start on Saturday. Dad, still in his pajama pants, drives me so I don't have to leave the Sportster in the school parking lot overnight. Much ado is made about seating choices on the bus, which is bigger and fancier than the school bus we usually take to shows. I'm torn between wanting to sit next to Jaz so we can hold hands under her jacket and sitting with Matty so I can nap. I end up with neither, because Alyssa's taking the bus this time and Jaz has to comfort Carina, who showed up this morning with red eyes and runny mascara. I'm not privy to the drama of Carina's inner life, so I find a seat several rows behind them and settle in. I try not to be bothered when no one ends up sitting beside me. This is what I want, right? To be left alone so I can listen to music and do my own thing?

Still, I can't stop my gaze from flitting up to Jaz and Carina every few minutes as the bus takes us out of Itaska. Jaz has confirmed the two of them are 100% platonic, and I believe her, but a petty part of me envies their closeness. I haven't had a best friend since Maria in elementary school, who made me a bracelet as a goodbye present that I promptly lost during the move from Texas to Ohio.

The bus stops once on the way, a gas station in the middle of nowhere with an Arby's attached. I cannot in good conscience put Arby's into my body, so I pick up a bottle of water and a slice of convenience store cheese pizza—as if that's better—and get in line at the register.

Jaz sidles up behind me with a bag of gummy worms. "What've you been listening to? It must have been good. You didn't notice the entire trumpet section singing '99 Bottles of Beer on the Wall.'"

"Oh, I noticed," I say. "I just chose not to respond. You see, when I was six, I trained under a Zen Buddhist master . . ."

She pushes my shoulder, giggling. "Stop it."

I shrug. "Who's to say it's not true? I'm an enigma.

I don't even know all my secrets."

I fish out some cash and pay for my lunch and Jaz's gummy worms.

"You don't have to do that," she protests.

"I want to."

She immediately caves, grinning as I hand her the candy. "Okay."

Jaz pops a gummy worm in her mouth as we head outside. "Anyways, I was gonna say you should take out your earbuds for a bit. The drive to Marshall's always interesting. I have it on good authority that Penny Grayson brought a full-on karaoke machine and plans to break it out for the second leg. Also the flutes have been sharing caramel corn, and I very much plan to mooch off them."

"I *am* a fan of caramel . . ."

"If anyone tries to make you sing, I'll cause a diversion. Scout's honor." She holds up three fingers with one hand, opening the door for me with the other. "What do you say?"

I can't resist Jaz when she makes puppy-dog eyes. Her irises look rich and golden in the sunlight. *A fan of caramel, indeed.*

"Fine, fine," I say. "Just stop making that face at me. It's making me want to do things I shouldn't be doing in public."

Her eyes light up with mischief. "Oh yeah? Like what?"

I glance around. No one's paying attention, since most are still waiting for the painfully slow Arby's employees to make their Piles o' Meat™. I divert course to the side of the convenience store. Jaz follows, holding a finger gun and acting like a super spy on a mission.

I lean against the wall and pull her in by the waist.

She stops humming the *Mission: Impossible* theme song and melts into me, eyelids heavy. Her lips lower toward mine, painfully slow, then stop only millimeters away. She's so close I can smell the candy on her breath.

When I groan in frustration, she smiles wickedly. "Sorry, Mathis. It's not Sunday. Shop's closed."

Jaz releases me and walks back toward the bus, hips swaying in her skintight leggings. I lay my head back on the stucco and run a hand over my face. This girl is going to be the death of me.

CHAPTER TWENTY

I TAKE JAZ'S advice and keep my earbuds out for the second leg of the bus ride. As predicted, there is caramel corn and a raucous round of karaoke. At one point, Michael gets in on the action, channeling his inner Justin Timberlake for a surprisingly good rendition of "Suit and Tie." He even manages to get Alvarez to sing along for a chorus, though she refuses to join in with his bus seat dance moves.

It's thirty minutes after the gas station when Sam Tan announces that he needs to pee.

"Sorry, buddy. Still an hour to go. Should've gone at the gas station." Alvarez's voice holds no pity.

"I *did* go at the gas station," Sam calls from his seat near the back. Quietly enough that our director can't hear it, he adds, "I also drank a thirty-two-ounce Mountain Dew at lunch, but so what?"

"Dude," his best friend, Garrett, says. "You should go out the window."

"*Dude,* I'm not a monster." He looks around at those of us who are nearby. "Hey, anybody got a bottle?"

There's a chorus of *ewww*s.

"I'm serious, guys. I really gotta go and Alvarez

isn't gonna stop! If I don't find a bottle, I am going to open this window and pee out of it. No cap," he finishes with solemnity.

Terrified that he's actually telling the truth, I fish in my bag until I find the empty water bottle from lunch. I get on my knees and toss it to him a few rows back.

"Don't spill," I say dryly.

A few people crack up at that, and I smirk to myself as I sit back down. Garrett holds up a towel from his backpack to shield everyone from the sight of Sam peeing. A glance toward the front tells me the leaders haven't noticed what's going on. There is no one to save us now.

A clarinet whispers, "Oh my god, he's doing it!"

When he's finished, Sam caps the bottle, opens the window, and tosses it out. Usually I wouldn't approve of littering like that, but in this case, I'm not about to complain.

***

DAD 9:50 PM
How'd the show go?

Kendall 9:52 PM
Not bad
Third place!

Dad 9:52 PM
Good job. Wish we could've come. Oma and Opa went to bed early and I'm stuck watching people make grilled cheese sandwiches out of waffles.

Kendall 9:53 PM
That doesn't sound so bad

Dad 9:54 PM
They're chocolate chip waffles.

Kendall 9:54 PM
Yikes
You going to bed soon?

Dad 9:56 PM
Soon. You too?

Kendall 9:57 PM
Just got to the gym, so probably soon for me too
Love ya

Dad 9:57 PM
Love ya too.

Marshall High School is putting us up on their basketball court for the night. The general vibe is a giant, out-of-control sleepover as everyone grabs sleeping bags and pads and pillows and yoga mats from the bottom of the coach bus.

"Three feet apart! That's all I'm asking," Alvarez shouts as everyone races to set up in clusters with their friends. "We have parent chaperones all over the place, so don't try anything. Lights out at midnight!"

I lay out my stuff between Matty and Jaz, with Carina on her other side. Near our heads, Emilio helps Alyssa set up a cot with a foam pad on top. Adam and his friends have found a corner and are currently playing the slap game, still-rolled sleeping bags abandoned in a pile.

I pull out the book we're being forced to read in English class. I'm way behind on it. Literary classic or not, *Heart of Darkness* is the absolute worst. I keep trying to slog through it, but I know I'm going to eventually give up and read a summary online.

Jaz and Carina have already set up their sleeping areas when they go back to the bus and come back with two enormous duffels full of more bedding.

I sit up, grateful for a distraction. "How could you possibly need all that?"

"You'll see." Jaz passes her spot and continues on to the nearest corner, where it's closed in on three sides by the bleachers, a wall, and the entrance to the locker room.

It's like she's a magnet. Out of nowhere, half a dozen other kids converge to help pull bedding from the bags. Jaz gets to work with a Ziploc of oversized clothespins, clipping sheets and duvets together and attaching them to whatever sticks out of the walls. Carina arranges pillows and cushions on the floor. It takes me way too long to realize what they're creating: a freaking giant blanket fort.

Jaz waves me over. "Come on! What are you waiting for?"

Everyone seems to know exactly what they're doing. I barely pin up one corner of a sheet before the duffels are empty and the fort is complete. Carina even strings up a set of twinkle lights on the inside, which is filled with comfy sitting areas. Lofi hip hop plays from a Bluetooth speaker by the door. It's kind of magical.

"Holy smokes," I breathe as I crawl inside. "This is amazing."

"Thanks," Jaz says. "It's my baby."

"Congrats! I didn't know you were expecting."

She rolls her eyes. "You know what I mean. Carina gets a little credit, too, although I brought the stuff for it freshman year." She leads me to a pile of pillows and flops down. I sit cross-legged beside her, my knee inches from hers. "That first year, it was just us and Carina's older sisters. But the next time, we invited a few of the other percs, and they invited others, and then last year it was basically half the band. As you can see," she gestures around us, "it's gotten even bigger this year. Our old director was cool with us doing it, so Alvarez tolerates the tradition."

People are still crawling through the door, some with pillows in hand or bags of snacks. Everyone's in leggings and sweats and nightgowns. Jaz has changed into a matching set of pinstriped pajamas, like something out of a movie, and she's so gosh darn cute I can hardly stand it.

"I like this," I say, gesturing to her pink and white button-up shirt.

"Thanks." She beams. "I brought them specifically for this. It's important to look your best on Fort Night."

Side by side, we people-watch and hum along to the music. A card game starts up, but I'm content to simply observe as Alyssa begins her reign of terror from a cushion by the entrance. No way I'm risking the red hands I see on people whenever they play a card-slapping game with her.

On the other end of the fort, the beginnings of a back-rub circle are forming.

Jaz points toward the group. "Want to?"

I swallow thickly. Do I have an ounce of self-preservation left?

Apparently not. I'm crawling and joining in before

I know what I'm doing. Jaz slots herself in the circle behind me. In front of me is a guy who I think plays tuba and whose name is possibly Dan. No one seems to care whom they're massaging—the personal bubble is a foreign concept in marching band.

Jaz smooths her hands over my back. "Where do you carry your tension?"

"My neck, I guess? And my shoulders."

She slides her hands up and starts kneading the muscles below the base of my skull. Her hands are strong from drumming, and the callouses on her fingers brush against my neck whenever she moves to a new knot. I hope she doesn't notice the goosebumps that immediately appear on my arms. Dan, on the other hand, is probably getting the worst back rub of his life. *Sorry, bud. I'm a little distracted.*

I feel my shoulders loosen as she works, slowly descending from their usual spot near my ears.

"Wow," I say. "Have you considered becoming a masseuse?"

Jaz laughs softly behind me. "My mom did massage school for a while. She had a lot of odd jobs before she settled on accounting. She's an . . . eclectic person when it comes to careers."

"Weird," I say. "I honestly would've pegged her for the stable one in your parents' marriage. Your dad seems more like the type to jump around."

"Naw, he's been in construction forever. Worked his way up, and now he manages big luxury builds in Minneapolis and stuff. Loves it too much to try anything else." Her hands are working beneath my shoulder blades now. "What do your parents do?"

The alarm bell in my head is so faint I can ignore it easily. "My mom does consulting in Colorado, some kind of PR stuff. I don't really get her job. I just know we moved a ton because of it. My dad's a car mechanic."

"Oh cool, is that why you're into motorcycles and stuff?" she asks.

I shrug. Jaz gently but insistently pushes my shoulders back down so she can keep massaging.

"We always used it as an excuse to get outside and away from the chaos of my siblings and mom," I say. "Just a time to be quiet and work with our hands and not be bothered by anyone. We don't do it quite as much now that we don't have anyone to escape from. And I've been busy with band. . . ."

I trail off, guilt tapering my words. When was the last time I worked on something with Dad? Not since we fixed up my bike before the first day of school. No wonder the man's stuck watching TV all the time.

"I'm sure he understands." Jaz's hands ease up on my back, not going for knots anymore, just a light relaxing pressure. "Senior year is a busy time."

"A regular dad would be fine. But mine has been through a lot the past couple of months. I feel responsible for him."

"Why?"

We're interrupted by Madison, who seems to be the boss of this particular massage circle. "Switch directions!"

I turn around, not making eye contact with my tuba massage partner. It's awkward, but if this is the social contract I must enter in order to touch Jaz in public, so be it. *Get those hands on me, Dan.*

I do a quick assessment of Jaz's shoulders and back, prodding with my thumbs to figure out where she has the most tension. The analytical part of my brain goes into problem-solving mode: start with her lower back, where the marching harness rests, then get her shoulders and arms, tight from drumming. If I have time, I'll get to her neck.

"Kendall?"

I've forgotten we're in the middle of a conversation, one that makes me feel nervous and raw. "Sorry. Yeah."

I get to work on the small of her back, and she hisses when I hit the knots. I apologize again.

"The divorce has been . . ." I struggle to find the right word. ". . . Messy. My mom did some stuff that really hurt him. I came out here with him so we could live with my grandparents, get him back on his feet. But I'm also fielding all these texts and calls from her. She wants to talk to dad; she wants to visit. I know seeing her would screw up any progress he's made so far. I deal with her stupid, wine-drunk ideas so he doesn't have to."

Jaz is silent for a minute. Even surrounded by a dozen sweaty teenagers, my senses are perfectly attuned to her cherry vanilla scent, faint as it may be. I'm like a freaking drug-sniffing dog when it comes to Jaz Whitaker.

"You sound like a really good daughter," Jaz finally says, her voice thoughtful. "Don't take this the wrong way, but I feel like you're taking on too much with your parents' situation. You're the oldest child, and you have this connection to your dad where you can feel all the pain he's going through, and you want to fix it. But you're still a kid. It's not fair for them to expect you to be the adult in this situation, taking care of your dad and managing your mom."

"None of it is fair."

"Of course not. But none of it is your fault, either. You realize that, right? Your parents made their choices, and now they have to deal with the consequences. They owe it to you and your siblings to be actual grown-ups and figure their crap out. *None* of that should fall on you."

My hands slow to a stop. I stare at the back of Jaz's neck, trying to process what she's saying. It makes sense, logically, but my mind can't seem to accept the reasoning. Every time I consider stepping out of my parents' drama, leaving them to hash it out themselves, I'm flooded with guilt and anxiety. What if things get worse because of me?

Jaz's phone lights up on the gym floor next to her. She taps it and reads something on the lock screen.

"Shoot. Carina."

The tempo of my pulse bumps up. "Is she okay?"

She turns her body halfway, cocks her head at me, and seems to make a decision. "Come on."

CHAPTER TWENTY-ONE

WE ABANDON OUR spots, forcing the massage circle to shrink its circumference to close the gap. I follow Jaz out of the blanket fort. Half the lights in the gym are off now, and the mood is muted and sleepy. Alvarez is set up under a basketball hoop, tapping away in the glow of a laptop screen. The other chaperones lounge on air mattresses and cots around the edges of the court. Some even look like they're asleep already.

"Thirty minutes till lights out," Michael calls from his spot beneath the other hoop. He's wearing glasses and is reading a tattered paperback.

Jaz salutes, then she leads me by the hand into the boys' locker room tucked behind our makeshift party tent. The door closes, muting the music and chatter from outside. We weave through lockers and benches until I hear it: a sniff, amplified by the echoey room.

We turn the corner to find Carina sitting on the floor of a shower stall, arms around her knees. When she sees us, she swipes beneath her eyes with the sleeve of her black, oversized hoodie.

"What is she doing here?" she croaks. There's no venom to it—her voice sounds flat, toneless.

Jaz plops herself next to Carina on the floor. She tucks an arm around her friend's shoulders, leaning their heads together. I stay up, feeling awkward, similarly confused as to why I've been dragged into all this.

"Is it for sure, then?" Jaz says, not answering Carina's question. "They're filing the papers?"

Carina swallows and nods, a few tears escaping down her face.

"That blows." Jaz's voice cracks, like she's genuinely sad, too. "I'm sorry, Care Bear."

She glances up at me, then, and dips her head meaningfully. I obey, slowly kneeling on the other side of Carina.

"Are your . . . parents getting divorced?" The reason I've been brought in here is starting to make sense.

She heaves a big sigh, filled with a mixture of resignation and sadness and only a hint of her usual disdain for me. "Yeah."

I work my tongue beneath my upper lip, contemplating what to say. We may not be besties, but I had this moment of my own not too long ago. Mom sat me down, just the two of us, and said she was filing for divorce from Dad. She wanted to tell me first so that I could break it to Jackson and Caylee. She knew I would be strong for them, she said. Strong for the whole family. I cried like this too, at first, but it was quickly replaced with a deep, simmering anger.

"At least now the fighting will probably stop," Jaz attempts. "Once they're separated, they can't yell at each other every night. That's kind of a silver lining, right?"

I cut her off. "Don't do that 'look at the bright side'

crap. No offense.”

“None taken,” she says, though the way she purses her lips makes me suspect there may have been *some* taken.

I turn to Carina, who’s staring at the drain set in the middle of the speckled tile. “I know I wasn’t in a place to look for silver linings when my parents told me they were splitting up. It just really, really sucked.”

Carina’s gaze flicks up, making eye contact with me for the first time since I entered the stall.

“Just got finalized,” I confirm. “That’s the reason I moved. My mom was cheating on my dad, and I found out.”

“That’s effed up,” she says, voice scratchy.

I laugh, no humor in it. “Yeah, it is. Parents are the worst.”

“Amen.”

I ignore Jaz’s eyes on me. She knew my parents were split up, but I hadn’t told her about the affair.

“I honestly don’t have anything comforting to say. I wish I did.” I smooth my hands on my thighs, uneasy being vulnerable with someone with such obvious distaste for me. But I know I can at least help her feel less alone. I can be the person *I* wish had been there when this happened to me. “Just know that your life isn’t over. This will hurt for a long time, but eventually you’ll come to terms with it. I think I’m starting to. But I’m still pissed off and sad and confused a lot of the time. It doesn’t fix what’s going on with your family, but know that you have somebody around who gets it.”

Carina clears her throat and wipes beneath her eyes again. “Thank you, Kendall. That honestly does kinda help.”

I sigh, finally settling in to sit next to the other two. "I'm glad, because I'm usually garbage at this kind of stuff. Jaz is the one all in touch with her feelings. She was just therapizing me about *my* whole situation."

"She's a good one," Carina agrees.

"Why are you talking about me in third person?" Jaz says.

I ignore her. "Yeah, she is. She *does* need to learn to let people wallow in their feelings sometimes, though. *Silver lining.* Ugh."

Carina cleans herself up, and the three of us walk together out of the locker room to help the others take down the blanket fort. Alvarez is fun enough to let us have it for a few hours, but she's not so naive as to leave it up all night.

Carina pulls me aside as everyone heads to bed. "Thank you, again, for talking me down in there. I know I haven't been the nicest to you since you moved here."

I shrug, even though it's true.

"I'll be straight-up with you," she continues in a low voice. "I was kind of jealous at first. Jaz has been my best friend for years, and when she got distracted by the shiny new girl, I was scared that I'd lose my spot in her life."

"I was never trying to replace you."

"I can see that now." She faces me head-on, a single finger lifted. "But I can also see what's happening between you and Jaz. I'd be a pretty crappy best friend if I didn't warn you—do *not* break my girl's heart."

CHAPTER TWENTY-TWO

EARLY ON IN the year, Jaz, Carina, and Emilio and I figured out we all have English class at the same time but with different teachers. Jaz the Overachiever is in AP, while I'm taking honors. Carina and Emilio are in the regular classes, but one grade apart since he's a junior.

A few weeks after the Marshall trip, we're walking together toward the English wing when I notice a new poster above the stairs.

GET YOUR HOMECOMING TICKETS NOW!

I'm about to continue walking, but Emilio stops to read the rest.

"'October 16th after the Itaska-McKinley football game. Theme: Timeless elegance.' What does that even mean?"

"It means everyone got too slutty at last year's HOCO, and they're trying to get out ahead of it," Jaz says. "Remember? Landon Prague got detention for jumping onstage to twerk on his boyfriend."

The three of them laugh, and I get a twinge of

envy that I don't have these shared experiences with everyone.

"Is homecoming big here?" I ask. "At my last school, only the football players and their girlfriends cared about it. I've never been."

"Oh yeah," Carina says. "People get all excited because it's less work than prom and it's the first dance where they crown royalty. Pretty cringe."

"You're just saying that because Braxton broke up with you two days before homecoming last year," Jaz says as we continue walking. "I think it's fun! *Especially* when people get detention for twerking. Do you think you'll go, Kendall?"

I shrug. "I'm with Carina. School dances are stupid. Just a chance to buy clothes you'll never wear again and pretend anything that happens in high school matters once you've graduated."

I glance at Jaz and realize her face has fallen. In fact, she looks a little panicky. When she catches me looking, she quickly smiles and returns to normal. I glance at the others, but Emilio's showing Carina a meme on his phone and they don't seem to have noticed. Jaz snatches the phone to get in on whatever's funny, and the moment passes.

Huh. That was weird.

We arrive at the common area, where the chaos of passing period reigns supreme. My locker is a few away from Emilio's, so he and I split off from the other two to grab some papers for our next class. Now that I can remember his name, we've gotten pretty chill with each other. He has good taste in music, so we swap recommendations sometimes. We're chatting about a local band he likes as I put in my locker combination. Right before I pull on the handle, I catch Jaz watching us from across the crowded room.

I open the door, and a half dozen balloons float out.

"Whoa!" I snatch the curly ribbon that ties them together before they float up to the high ceiling. The balloons are all different colors, a sudden rainbow marquee flashing the message, *"Look at me!"* I tug them down to the relative privacy beneath the top of the lockers. "What is going on?"

Emilio bends over to poke at a blue balloon. "Look, there are papers inside."

I fish a pen from my locker and hold it up the first balloon, then hesitate. "I probably shouldn't pop a balloon in a crowded room, should I?"

Emilio frowns. "Probably not. Here, I've got it."

He takes the balloon and bites a tiny hole near the knot, and the air leaks from it with a squeal.

"Good thinking."

"Thanks! I twist balloons on the weekends for some extra cash."

"*How* did I not know that about you?"

He shrugs. "Never asked."

The balloon finishes deflating. I use my pen to rip the hole open wider, then I reach in and pull out a little rolled piece of paper bearing the word "YOU."

Dread sparks inside me. "Oh, this better not be what I think it is."

We systematically deflate each balloon and pull out the rest of the papers. Sure enough, they bear the words HOMECOMING, WILL, GO, ME?, WITH, and TO.

I sit back against the bank of lockers and groan. A few people have stopped to watch, giggling and whispering. I pop up to my feet and look toward

Jaz's locker. She's watching me intently, but there's no mistaking the hopeful tilt of her eyebrows.

I point at her, then me, and jerk my thumb toward the benches by the cafeteria. *You. Me. Talk.*

***

JAZ LOOKS PENITENT as she takes a seat next to me on the semi-secluded cafeteria table. I put on my sternest face and fold my hands.

"Jaz," I say. "Are you asking me to homecoming?"

"Yes." She looks up at me through long, dark lashes and bites her lower lip.

Focus, Mathis.

I tap my foot on the ground, trying to think of the best way to approach this. "I thought . . . I don't know. I thought we were going to be more low-key. Going to homecoming together seems like a pretty big public statement." An upsetting thought occurs to me. "This isn't about the bet, is it?"

"What bet?"

"What b—the bet we've been doing this whole time! The one where you try to make me love this place!"

"I thought the fact that we kissed kind of negated that whole thing. Wasn't that what the whole thing was about for you?"

"No. Yes. I don't know." I want to bang my head on the table. "Couldn't we have talked about this first? What subliminal message was I sending that you interpreted to mean, 'Please ask me to homecoming?'"

"I don't know, maybe the fact that we have a standing date to feel each other up every Sunday?" she retorts, perfect eyebrows arched with indignation. "And you get along with my brother and my parents like they're your own family? Maybe because my mom started calling you 'Kenny' and you haven't once told her to stop? And that you watch football with us and scream at the screen even though I *know* you're not into sports?"

I clutch at the roots of my hair, wishing I could rewind the past hour. "I'm sorry! I do like going to your house and hanging with your family and . . . *feeling you up.*" I say the last part in a harsh whisper. "This has been pretty much the best month of my life. But I can't . . . I don't . . ."

I wish my stupid mouth would say the right words. I want to tell her that she's perfect and there's no way I can be enough for her. That she deserves everything good in the world, and I'm just messed up and mediocre. "Jaz, I'm scared."

"Are you scared because it's with a girl? Is that what this is about?"

"No," I say emphatically. "I'm not ashamed of going with a girl. It's just a big step, and I'm not ready to take it. Can't we all go as a group? Isn't that a normal thing to do?"

Jaz folds her arms as the warning bell rings, meaning we have two minutes left to get to our next class. "So you're not ashamed of being queer. You're ashamed of me."

"I—am not—ashamed—of you." I emphasize the statement with my fist on the table. "I just have stuff to work through. There's a lot going on with my family, you know?"

"No, I don't know!" she bursts out. "Because you barely ever talk about them! You're basically part of my family, and I've never even met your dad or grandparents. I only found out about your mom's affair because you were telling Carina. I don't know where you live. I hardly know anything about your brother and sister. But I want to. I want to know *you,* every part of you, but you keep yourself hidden away."

My jaw tightens. "I have to get to class. We can't have this conversation right now. I think we should go to homecoming as friends, with everyone else. Think about it."

I pick up my books and head to chemistry.

***

JAZ GHOSTS ME until the next day, when I wake up to a text on my phone. She must have gotten up early for a morning run.

DJ Jazzy Jeff 6:12 AM

Fine. I'll go as friends. But if you're really not ashamed of being queer, you should take another girl as your date.

Kendall 7:01 AM

What the heck is that going to solve

DJ Jazzy Jeff 7:05 AM

You should ask Sarah Lockhart. Don't you have a class together?

We do track together, and she's super nice and definitely gay. I bet she'd say yes.

Kendall 7:07 AM

I hardly know her

We've spoken like two words to each other in woodshop

DJ Jazzy Jeff 7:08 AM

Just ask. She's chill.

I fume all morning. Why doesn't Jaz believe me when I tell her I'm not ashamed? It's like I'm a piece of music for her, something she has to get perfectly right or else there's no point in trying. What she doesn't get is that I'm all mixed up, nothing in the right key, a million different tempos. She can't memorize me and play me back however she wants.

I ride to school with grim determination. *Fine. If she wants me to ask Sarah, I'll ask Sarah.* If only to prove to Jaz that I care.

We're working on making a bookcase from scratch in woodshop. When Sarah goes to pick out stain from the paint shelf, I follow her.

"Hey," I say in a half-whisper, looking around to make sure no one's listening to us.

"Hey." She doesn't look weirded out, just friendly and curious about what I have to say. That's a good sign.

I can do this. "I was wondering . . . would you like to go to homecoming together? Like, casually. I think it could be fun."

She's quiet for a moment, contemplating the labels on a can in front of her. "As friends?"

"Yeah! Exactly. I know a bunch of people going in a group. I just thought it'd be cool to have a date, since it's our senior year homecoming and everything."

Sarah pulls a stain off the shelf and shoots me a smile. "Sure, that sounds fun. Do we need to coordinate our outfits or get corsages or anything?"

"Not unless you want to."

"Are you kidding? I hate that stuff. Okay if I wear a suit?"

"Absolutely."

And that's that. It was easier than I thought it would be, and Sarah seems like she's genuinely looking forward to it. The only thing bad is that now I have to find something to wear.

CHAPTER TWENTY-THREE

DAD'S SIDE OF the family has never known a thing about fashion. My mother, despite all her flaws, is a fantastic dresser. Even I can admit her style is good, business casual with just enough edge to make her stand out. Her pixie cut flatters her face perfectly, and she keeps it dyed a natural-looking shade of red. She even did a little bit of modeling before she and Dad got married.

Desperate times call for desperate measures. I swallow my pride and reach out to her.

Kendall 6:58 PM
Can you help me with something clothes-related?

Mom 7:49 PM
Of Course!!1!

Kendall 7:55 PM
I need something to wear to the homecoming dance

Mom 7:57 PM

Oh that's right, homecoming is coming up! So exciting. I have so many Memories. Wish I could be there

I wait, but that's all she sends. I scrub a hand over my face. *Come on, Mom. It's a weekday. Lay off the wine.*

Kendall 8:11 PM
  Any ideas for an outfit?? I'm desperate

Despite being tipsy, she manages to send me three links to dresses on Amazon. The first two are more her style than mine, too professional for a high school dance. The last one is okay—even I can admit that. It's a sleeveless black skater dress with a hem that reaches mid-thigh and a cutout on the back. I kind of wish she'd sent me something more edgy. If I were more invested in this, I might even push for a suit. I feel like I could rock that. But I'm *not* invested in this, and the black dress is fine. I'm already logged into Mom's account, so I hit order before I can change my mind.

Things with Jaz have been polite but distant since the balloon debacle. There hasn't been any more kissing, unfortunately. I hang with Adam, who's excited for his upcoming birthday, and Jaz treats me like any other visitor. She seems genuinely glad that I'm going to homecoming with Sarah, though.

"You need to get to know people outside of band," she tells me the Friday before the dance.

We're standing outside the fieldhouse, waiting to line up for the band's homecoming pep rally performance. Most of us are in uniform, but Jaz is in her dress for the dance because she's been nominated as homecoming royalty. It's a strapless gown with sequins on the bust that start teal, then flow down in an ombre gradient to a white, gauzy skirt that hits right above her knees. She's taken down her twists, leaving a voluminous mane of tiny, perfect coils that she's styled in a deep side part.

She has her snare harness on over her outfit. She insists on marching out with the band even though she'll have to split off to stand with the other nominees before we perform the fight song. Guess she can't trust anyone else to play the cadence.

I change the subject from my social life. "Think you're going to win queen?"

Jaz lets out a short laugh. "Ha! There's no way. I'm splitting the band votes with Madison and the athlete votes with Emma Bissett."

Jaz says her ex's name dismissively, like she's not even worth a second thought. I've never spoken to Emma, only seen her in the hallways. She's my height but much thinner, and she moves with the muscular grace of someone who can launch herself into the air with a pole and not die. Her lip piercing and perfectly wavy hair don't help, either. They're both things I wish I could pull off, and she rocks them.

Jaz's prediction is half-right. She stands next to Madison, whose strapless, sparkly dress is as short as the school will allow, if not slightly shorter. Last year's homecoming queen hovers the crown over each nominee's head while Carina plays a drum roll, culminating in a late cymbal crash from the sophomore cymbal player as the crown is placed on Emma Bissett's head.

***

I DON'T USUALLY help Oma in the shop until it's

closed, but when she asks me to bring a few boxes down to the workshop before I leave for the homecoming game, I don't think twice. Her knees have been bugging her, and Opa and Dad are busy grabbing takeout for a quick family dinner before I have to go.

"Where do you want them?" I grunt.

She points to a stack of plastic cases filled to bursting with Disney piano books and violin learners. I carefully balance the boxes on top of the cases, shocked as always that this woman manages to run a successful business. I should be a little easier on her, though. The shop reorganization is nearly complete, and with mine and Dad's help, Schultz Music is looking better than ever.

I'm about to go back and get ready for the game when the bell on the door rings. I head toward the front before Oma can move. "I'll help them. You hang out."

I see a head of black hair peeking above the shelf of lyres and sheet music. I notice the streaks of green too late—the person turns the corner, and I'm face-to-face with Carina. I freeze like a deer in headlights. Her mouth pops open, and we stand there, staring at each other. She's the first to break the spell.

"Hey, Kendall," she says. "Fancy meeting you here."

Why didn't I find out who it was before I showed my face? At least she thinks I'm a customer. Maybe I can spin this like I did with Jaz.

"Oh, uh, yeah," I say, trying to act natural. "I love this place. I get all my, uh, reeds here."

"Cool." She gives me side-eye as she turns to a shelf of drumsticks and peruses the options. "Broke a stick, so I figured I'd stop by on my way to the school. Hey, do you know where the owner is? She always has good recommendations.”

“Uh, yeah.” Dying inside, I wave my hand toward the desk where I left Oma, not turning to face it.

“Thanks.” She disappears toward the back of the shop.

I pretend to examine a didgeridoo while Carina greets Oma.

“Hello, young lady,” she says. “Was my granddaughter not able to help you? I tell you, I can never get good help anymore.”

Oh no. *Oh no.*

“Your granddaughter?” Carina asks, still using the polite voice I’ve noticed she only reserves for adults.

“Yes, Kendall,” Oma says like Carina’s simple in the head. “Didn’t I hear you talking to her over there? She’s my son’s daughter. Have you met her? She goes to Itaska High.”

“Yeah, I have.” I can’t see Carina’s face, but she speaks slowly and thoughtfully, like she’s figuring it all out. “We know each other pretty well, actually. I didn’t realize she was related to you.”

Oma helps her pick out a good pair of drumsticks. I’m still frozen in my spot by the didgeridoos when Carina leaves, casting me a weird look as she goes.

Well, that’s just perfect. I have no doubt Jaz is going to hear about this, and I’m sure she’ll make the connection to the time we came here together and I pretended not to know Opa. Why did I even feel like I had to keep this place secret from everybody? It was stupid, and now a tiny lie has turned into a whole thing that’s only going to make Jaz *and* Carina upset with me. I’ve already got all this homecoming stuff to balance, which is precarious enough as it is. Jaz has pretended she’s fine that her ex got crowned queen, but I can tell it threw her off. And I'm still not sure I made the right choice asking Sarah to be my date. It was Jaz's suggestion, but I can't shake the feeling I've made a mistake.

Now Carina has dirt on me. Just another thing to add to the pile, I guess.

I'm going to be late if I don't hurry and get ready. Opa and Dad walk in through the back door as I take the apartment stairs two at a time to grab my show bag. I'm just walking out of my room when my phone rings.

"Hey, Mom. Can't talk long—I'm late for a performance."

"Hey, sweetie! Are you at home?"

"Why?"

"I've got a big surprise for you. Don't be mad, but the kids and I just flew in to Minneapolis. We're here for homecoming weekend!"

CHAPTER TWENTY-FOUR

I SUFFER THROUGH the homecoming game, trying not to look at the stands where Mom, Jackson, and Caylee are seated next to Dad, Opa, and Oma. Oma has placed herself in the center of the group, by her grandkids, with Mom on one end and Dad on the other. Dad spends a large amount of the game with his elbows on his knees and his head hanging down.

On the phone, I managed to convince Mom to get a hotel room instead of cramming everyone into Oma's house. My feelings are all over the place: excitement to see Jackson and Caylee in person after months away, anger at Mom for springing this on us, worry for Dad's state of mind. Add to that everything with Jaz, and I'm surprised I make it through our performance on the field plus two hours of pep band without passing out.

I'm determined to skip out on the band the second we get back inside after the game. I get changed, gather up my stuff, and practically sprint out the exit, but Adam catches up to me.

"Still good for Puzzle Sunday this week?"

"Of course," I reply, distracted while I look around for my family. "Wouldn't miss it."

"Kendall." I look down, and he quirks an eyebrow at me. "Why are you acting so weird? Is everything okay?"

I sigh. "Yeah, everything's fine. Just feeling a little off today."

"Want a hug? That always works for me when I'm feeling off." He shoots me a toothy smile. *This kid.*

"Come here, you." I squish Adam into a hug, because why not? My whole life is about to blow up. Might as well get a good hug out of it. I release him and give him an affectionate pat on the head. "You know, that did make me feel a little better. Thanks, man."

I watch Adam skip back into the school, heart feeling a little warm and fuzzy. I'm jealous of how optimistic the kid always seems to be. Life seems simpler for people who can make the best out of everything.

"Kendall!"

I'm attacked with another hug, this time from the direction of the parking lot. I look down to see my attacker—Caylee, my twelve-year-old sister. Two hugs in one day would usually be too much, but not when it comes to this. I squeeze her back, embarrassed when tears immediately rise into my eyes.

"I missed you so much, Cay," I choke out. "It's so good to see you."

Her chestnut brown hair is tied in pigtails with blue and gold ribbons, and attempts with a curling iron have left the ends just barely curly instead of straight. She's even applied swipes of blue eyeshadow and shaky wingtip eyeliner. *My heart.* I give her one more squeeze for good measure.

The others have made it over now. Jackson stays

behind, too cool for hugs, but Mom sweeps in and clutches me to her chest.

"I know you don't like surprises, but I couldn't resist the chance to see my daughter play at my alma mater." She smells like perfume and football concessions and plane sweat. No wine on her breath, at least.

"Hey, Mom." I feel like if I say anything more, I'll yell at her.

I pull away and offer my fist to Jackson. "Hey, little bro."

He slouches forward to give the laziest, most pathetic fist bump I've ever received in my life. A grunt comes from his mouth that could be interpreted as a "Hey" back. *The puberty is strong with this one.* He glances down at his phone, hair falling into his eyes. It's longer and shaggier than I'm used to, bleached from days spent longboarding in the sun. I want to reach up and tousle it, but I also want to live.

I step back to take in my entire family, back in one place for the first time in a long time: Opa, Oma, Dad, Mom, Jackson, and Caylee. It's bizarre to see them here, on the steps of Itaska High, all together. Like something out of *The Twilight Zone.*

"Anyone up for ice cream?" Mom says, oblivious to the awkwardness of the situation. "We *have* to go to Charlie's. It was always my favorite place to go after football games."

"Charlie's shut down." Oma's voice is flat. She's making no secret of her displeasure at Mom's sudden appearance back in the life of her son—the same son Mom cheated on and divorced a few months ago.

Dad, on the other hand, hasn't spoken a word. He gives me a small, strained smile when I meet his eyes. This isn't good for him, I'm positive. Mom's only here till Monday, though. *Let's just get through this,* I try to tell him without words. *It's only till Monday.*

***

IN THE MIDST of the weirdest weekend of my life, I put on a dress, wedge heels, and more makeup than I usually wear. I had been planning to add just eyeliner to my usual mascara and lipstick, but Mom insisted on giving my face a full contour with makeup she brought in her suitcase. That's Mom, always *insisting.* I fume while she finishes the blush on my cheeks, and I fume while Oma takes pictures of me and laments that I won't bring my date by for a couple's photo.

I can't get out of the house and into Dad's car fast enough. I figure Sarah won't want to get picked up with a motorcycle, and with the absolute clown show going on at my home right now, I would rather die than have her come pick me up. At a stop light, I fluff my freshly curled hair and put on a pair of mini hoop earrings.

Sarah's house is perfectly normal, a white split-level in a neighborhood not far from the school. Her parents are friendly and her two young brothers heckle her as we take pictures in the front room. She's put her hair up in a messy bun, and she's wearing a navy-blue suit that fits her perfectly.

"You look really nice," I say as we walk to my car.

"Thanks," she responds. "You, too. Where'd you get your dress?"

"My mom found it online."

"She's got great taste."

I frown. "Yeah, I guess."

We pull up to the House of Cheesecake where

we're supposed to meet everyone else for dinner. The waitress shows us to the table we reserved. It's already occupied by Jaz, now wearing dangly pearl earrings and a full face of makeup, and a girl I've never seen. The girl's hair is long, black, and shiny, with glamorous waves that could be from a blowout or just fantastic genes. Her green dress looks expensive and way too classy for a high school dance.

"Hi, guys." Sarah says, taking a seat beside the stranger. "How's it going?"

"Great." Jaz's eyes flick up and down my outfit as I move to her side of the table. I suddenly wish I'd gone for something more elegant.

"Long time, no see," the black-haired girl says to Sarah. To me, she says, "I'm Rumiko. I go to Blaine."

I sit down across from Sarah. "Ah, got it. And you're here because . . . you know Sarah?"

"I'm here because I'm Jaz's date," she says with a smile.

My heart shrivels in my chest. "You're Jaz's date?" I didn't know *Jaz's* having a date was part of the plan. For some reason, it feels a whole lot worse than my taking my own date to this dance. At least with Sarah, we both know where we stand. This gorgeous human being in front of me was *not* part of the plan.

"Yup," Jaz says brightly. "Rumiko's my biggest competition on the track." I watch her face for hints of feelings, admiration, *anything,* but the girl is a brick wall tonight.

Huh. So Jaz brought a date to homecoming. I try to play it off. I shouldn't be surprised—it's not like I was going to let her go with me. Why shouldn't she have someone to be with tonight? I don't own her. She's amazing and beautiful and anyone would be lucky to take her to a dance.

I say that all in my head, but my stomach doesn't agree. We haven't even eaten, yet I feel like hurling.

The rest of our group arrives: Carina, Matty, Gavin, and Madison. Emilio brings Alyssa in, and he's wearing a bright blue tie the exact shade of her lacy dress. *Interesting.* It seems like the Marshall trip may have worked its charms again. I assumed she had a thing for Matty, but I guess I fell into the heteronormative trap of believing guys and girls can't be best friends without having secret feelings for each other.

The boys clap each other on the backs and start comparing boutonnieres with surprisingly specific knowledge about flower types and arrangements. Meanwhile, I'm left to make small talk with Sarah and Carina, who's sitting on my other side. I can't tell if she's told Jaz about seeing me in Schultz Music, but she's definitely treating me like we never had our breakthrough in the locker room. I'm back to a person she tolerates because we're in the same friend group, nothing more. On my right, Jaz is deep in conversation with her date.

The waitress arrives, and I bury myself in the menu she hands me. I try not to breathe a sigh of relief. What was I thinking, inviting someone I hardly knew to go on a long, drawn-out date with me? Sarah is nice enough, but I'm already struggling to come up with topics to talk about, and we haven't even gotten our sodas yet.

When I invited Sarah to homecoming, I offered to pay for everything, but she told me she was perfectly fine with going Dutch. When the waitress returns, I order a falafel salad and Sarah asks for the spinach lasagna.

"Are you vegetarian, too?"

Sarah chuckles. "I'm actually not, I just like spinach a lot. I know, weird. But no worries, I won't judge you if you don't judge me. How'd you become vegetarian?"

I have an answer to this, the one I've used for years. I launch into the story of living next-door to a family with chickens when I was a kid. I loved chasing them, learned all their names and everything. I was horrified when the neighbors had us over for dinner one night and the teenage son whispered to me that we were eating *Kevin*.

Sarah laughs at all the right moments in my story, and I begin to relax. She turns out to be fun to talk to once the ice is broken, and I barely notice time has passed until our food gets brought out. For a place named after a dessert, the falafel is honestly not bad. I'm too full to get my own dessert afterward, but Sarah lets me snitch a bite of the brownie she orders. By the time everyone loads up in their respective cars to go to the dance, my date and I are a lot more comfortable with each other.

"Where did you live before you moved here?" Sarah asks as I pull onto the highway in the direction of the school.

My jaw's clenched because I hate merging. I have to consciously relax my muscles before I can say, "Colorado."

"Oh wow, seriously?" She sounds genuinely excited. "I grew up in Colorado! My dad was stationed at the Air Force Academy south of Denver. Where'd you live?"

"Colorado Springs." I don't really want to get into talking about it more, but I can tell I've struck on something Sarah's actually interested in talking about.

"No way," she says. "We were right by the Springs. Did you ever go to Garden of the Gods? I loved renting an electric bike with my family and cruising around the whole place. Did you ever hike the Manitou Incline?"

And so it goes for the rest of the drive: Sarah chattering about Colorado and all her memories there, and me trying to answer politely but also not reveal that my mom and siblings still live there because my family is broken and my mom's a horrible person. I try not to heave an audible sigh of relief when I finally pull into the parking lot and the Colorado conversation is broken as we get out of the car together and walk inside the school.

Everyone else has beaten us there, probably because when not on a motorcycle I drive like a grandma. The group hasn't gone down to the dance floor yet, but Jaz bobs to the music as she talks anyway. Her hair looks incredible in a twist out, and the curls bounce every time she moves. I'm subject to the full effect of Jaz's outfit, too. Her teal and white dress sparkles in the lights coming from the dance floor, and she's swapped her usual sneakers for heels that accentuate the long, toned muscles of her calves. I have to force myself to look away.

I stare at the cafeteria instead, which has had all the tables pushed to the walls. The decorations are old-school Hollywood, I guess going with the "timeless elegance" theme, and there's a DJ with a purple afro spinning tunes at the front of the room. We've made sure to arrive fashionably late, so the dance floor is already packed with bodies.

My throat tightens at the sight of a hundred teenagers writhing in a crowded mass on the linoleum. Did I really forget until now that I'm allergic to crowds?

Jaz surveys the scenes and announces, "Well, what are we waiting for? Let's dance!"

I follow the group like I'm being sent to the gallows. The DJ's playing some cheesy pop ballad sped up with an ear-splitting 808 drum layered underneath. It's horrendous, but everyone in the group starts dancing, so I try to groove to the music a little bit so I don't look like a party pooper.

Eventually a less terrible song comes on. I loosen up, starting to enjoy myself as Sarah, Carina, and Matty dance around me. That is, until I see that Jaz and Rumiko have separated themselves and are dancing together . . . and pretty close, too.

I split off to get some punch with Sarah. We chat by the refreshment table. I try to get into our conversation, but I keep one eye on Jaz and Rumiko at all times. Sarah makes a somewhat funny comment and I laugh too loudly, throwing back my head for good measure. Jaz responds by moving a step closer to her date, shouting something in her ear as they bounce to the music.

The song changes into one I have heard many, many times: the Cupid Shuffle. I know every single move to the stupid dance that goes with it, mostly because Caylee had a line dance phase in sixth grade. Caught up in the loud music and weird competitiveness and dreamlike quality of the whole weekend, I grab Sarah's hand and drag her into the mass of people that have already start doing the moves.

To the right . . . To the left . . . Now kick . . .

Through it all, I dance extra flirty, making sure to cast smiles at Sarah every now and then as I swivel my hips. Jaz and Rumiko end up right next to us, and Jaz, too, is making the Cupid Shuffle more suggestive than it has any right to be. I turn up the dial on the sexiness of my dancing, and pretty soon we're in some sort of passive-aggressive contest for who can turn an innocent line dance into something NSFW.

Finally, the song ends. I'm out of breath from dancing so hard. Sarah's laughing, Rumiko's laughing, and Jaz sends me a death glare as I clap with everyone else and wipe the sweat off my forehead.

I'm drunk on ticking her off. That's the only explanation for why I lead Sarah off the dance floor and toward a set of lockers in the common area, where the music is only blaring instead of ear-splitting.

"I'm having a really good time!" I shout, leaning close so she can hear me.

"Me, too!"

"I'm glad we did this!"

Sarah smiles, and it's not the shy, polite kind that she usually gives when someone talks to her in woodshop. She's having a good time, and so am I. I glance at the dance floor—Jaz is looking our way. Possessed by some kind of demon, I make a split-second decision.

I put a hand on Sarah's shoulder and lean forward.

Sarah jerks away. "What are you doing?"

I'm left stranded in mid-air, my lips already puckered. I quickly stand straight and smooth out my hair. "Uh, I thought . . . I thought you wanted me to kiss you."

"I'm sorry if I gave you that idea, but . . ." Sarah groans and shakes her hands out, obviously upset. "Jaz is gonna kill me, but I've got to tell you. This isn't fair to anybody."

The music dims in my ears, distant and echoing, like we're at the end of a long tunnel. "What isn't fair to anybody?"

She spins around in a circle of frustration. "Argh! This is idiotic. I never should've agreed to this. So . . . don't freak out, but Jaz talked to me before you asked me to homecoming. She wanted me to say yes because I wasn't a threat. She knew I already had a girlfriend . . . Rumiko."

"Rumiko," I repeat, head swimming. Jaz is full-on staring at us from the dance floor, but her gorgeous date is still swaying her hips, not yet aware of what's going on. "Rumiko is your girlfriend? I don't understand."

"I don't really, either . . . but I owed Jaz a favor. She covered for me when I had to miss a track-and-field meet last year. It's a wild story—you should ask her sometime." She looks sheepish, arms folded in front of her, more like the timid version of herself I met at the beginning of the year. "Right after you ask her why she set this all up."

I don't know what else to say to Sarah. My face burns, embarrassed about how I've been acting when this has all been set up from the start. I'm angry at her, angry at myself for trying to kiss her to make Jaz jealous, and I'm *definitely* angry at Jaz. I spin on my heel, a clean pivot that would have Michael proud if I did it in rehearsal. Jaz is completely still, ready for my attack. I stalk toward her.

Rumiko seems to melt away into the crowd, leaving only Jaz and me as everyone gyrates around us. The music has gotten significantly darker and dirtier, and the dancing has transitioned to match. Do they not play any slow dances at this thing?

Where are the parent chaperones, for god's sake? I'm surprised twerking on a boyfriend was the worst thing someone got in trouble for last year.

"Are you serious right now?" I shout over the music. "Sarah and Rumiko are dating?"

"I can explain," Jaz starts.

I cut her off. "Do you know how messed up this is? How embarrassed I feel right now? If not, let me enlighten you. Right now, I feel like I got dressed up in this stupid outfit, then went out to dinner and a dance with a bunch of people who were laughing at me the whole time. Does everyone else know? Carina? Matty? I feel like a complete idiot."

"No!" Jaz waves her hands like she's trying to erase it all. "Nobody knows."

"Except Sarah and Rumiko."

"Except them. I wasn't even going to go through with it! I changed my mind. I was gonna call it all off yesterday, but then Carina told me about seeing you at Schultz."

Freaking Carina. I knew she would snitch. We can bond over crappy parents all we want, but when there was a chance to get between Jaz and me, she took it. I flip her off behind my back, where I know she's watching. Probably having the time of her life.

"Why did you have to lie about something stupid like who your grandparents are?" Jaz hugs her body, eyes tearing up. "I feel like I don't even know you. No matter what I do, you won't let me know you."

"You're one to talk! You tricked me into taking someone with a *girlfriend* to homecoming. And for what? To make me jealous? To prove that I'll do whatever you want, like all your other friends?" I feel queasy, realizing that Jaz has manipulated me, just like Mom is always doing. The lying, the need for control: it's straight out of the Miriam Mathis playbook. "Carina, Emilio, Matty—the entire band hangs onto your every word, but you don't even have the courage to stay up on the podium and actually *lead* them. Because that might reveal you're not as perfect as they think you are."

I'm shaking, infused from head to toe with hurt and indignation as we have it out in the middle of the cafeteria, shouting over an Imagine Dragons remix.

"You're an asshole!" Jaz starts to turn away, tears glinting in the strobe light.

"You're a control freak!" I yell after her. She stops but doesn't turn around. "Just answer this one thing. Why would you go to all this trouble? What's the point of it all?"

Because things haven't gotten dramatic enough, the music abruptly switches into the first slow song of the night right when Jaz shouts, "Because I need you to realize how you feel about me!"

Everyone near us snaps out of their hormone-fueled haze to stare at us. I barely notice. All the noise and the colors and the lights fade until there is a single pinpoint of Jaz in front of me, chest heaving.

"Well, congratulations," I say. "I guess I have."

Then I stalk past her and out of the room.

CHAPTER TWENTY-FIVE

JACKSON 10:46 AM
Left for the alumni brunch without you. Oma said not to wake you up. Now you have plenty of time to hang out with your new family.

Kendall 11:31 AM
Wtf are you talking about

Jackson 11: 33 AM
Your new little brother. That kid you were hugging at the football game

Kendall 11:39 AM
He's not my new brother, idiot
We just do puzzles on Sundays at his house

Jackson 11:40 AM
Real creative. From LEGO Sunday to Puzzle Sunday.

Kendall 11:40 AM
?????

Why is everyone being so stupid about everything?

Jackson 11:45 AM

Some of us care about our family. We don't just pick up and leave when things get hard.

Kendall 11:47 AM

I left Colorado because Mom cheated on Dad, okay?? They didn't want to tell you guys, but someone has to.

Jackson 11:48 AM

Yeah. We know. Mom told us like a month ago.

I slam my phone onto the bed so I don't throw it across the room. Are you kidding me? Why does no one communicate in this freaking family? I thought my little brother and sister were still blissfully ignorant to the whole cause for this divorce. Meanwhile, they casually knew, and no one thought to tell me.

Kendall 11:55 AM

Well then what's the problem here?
I left so I could support Dad
Not to abandon you guys

Jackson 11:59 AM

It's not the fact that you left. It's that you forget about everyone in your life the second they're out of sight. On to the shiny new thing. New state, new friends, new family.

"Ughhhh!" I scream into my pillow.

Of *course* I've managed to tick Jackson off, too. My skull feels like it's being hammered from within, an emotional hangover from my disastrous night. My family has ditched me for some French toast, and my brother's pissed off at me for, what? Being friendly with a boy close to his age?

I get out of bed to pee, but there's little reason to change out of the gym shorts and shirt I grabbed off the floor to sleep in when I got home last night. I'm pretty sure if I showed up at the Whitakers', Jaz would greet me at the door with a flamethrower. She tried to call twice last night, but I let them both go to voicemail. There's been nothing from her since.

As if on cue, a text from Adam appears.

Adam (Band) 11:51 AM
Are you coming today?

Kendall 11:53 AM
Don't know if I'm in the mood, sorry bud

Adam (Band) 11:53 AM
Are you sure? I could bring the puzzles to your house, if you don't wanna come here!!

Kendall 12:02 PM
Sorry
Just really not feeling it

It's my first Sunday not spent at the Whitakers' since Puzzle Sundays began. Dad has the car, and there's freezing rain outside, so I can't take the bike out anyway. And I'm not exactly in the mood for puzzles. I know exactly what type of mood I'm in.

I go to the cupboards first. It takes some searching, but I eventually hunt down the marshmallow creme spread, peanut butter, and bread. I slather the creme as thick as possible, with only a thin layer of peanut butter on the other side. Go big or go home, right?

I pour myself a glass of flat Coke Zero from the fridge and bring my ungodly brunch creation to the coffee table in the living room. I grab the throw blanket from a basket in the corner, curl up, and turn on *Great American Grilled Cheese Showdown*.

***

I MUST FALL asleep at some point, because when I wake up, the auto-play is already at episode three. I groan and find the remote, then turn off the TV and stretch my arms. I have two missed texts from Jaz.

DJ Jazzy Jeff 1:08 PM
Good job ruining Adam's birthday, moron
The only thing he wanted to do was eat cake with us and do a puzzle with you

My heart drops. *That's* what I was forgetting. I'd bought him a present, the puzzle I'd had my eye on at the local game store. But I've been so caught up in Mom's surprise visit and everything with Jaz that I completely forgot about it.

I drop back onto the couch, groaning. Outside, the freezing rain has stopped, but the sky is gray and lifeless.

"You and me both," I croak, mouth dry from sleeping with it wide open.

"What's that?" comes a voice from the kitchen.

I screech and fall off the couch. Opa appears from

around the corner, looking down at me with hands on his hips.

"What are you doing on the floor?" His little old man voice is gentle but teasing.

He helps me up with a soft-skinned hand. My heart's still pounding with the shock of waking up to what I thought was a home intruder.

"You scared me, Opa," I say. "I didn't know you guys were home!"

"The others are still down in the store. Oma wanted to show the kids the remodel, but I came up to get a snack." He pats his belly, clothed in a plaid button-up shirt tucked into too-high slacks. "They don't feed you nearly enough at those things."

"Might I recommend peanut butter and marshmallow creme?"

I move into the kitchen with my blanket and slump into a chair while Opa makes a sandwich and some tea. He doesn't speak again until he's seated across from me.

"Now," he says, pushing a mug of tea to my side. "Tell me what's got you sleeping in until noon."

"Everyone hates me."

"Everyone?"

"Well, Jackson does. And then half my friends at school, and there's this girl—"

"Ah, yes. Jasmine."

"How do you know that?"

"She's a very nice girl," he says with his mouth full. "Comes into the shop a lot. You were with her and made me pretend not to know you, remember?"

I rub my temples. "Yeah, that's the one."

"I figured you were embarrassed of us. I pick up on these things."

"I'm not—" I sigh, not sure how to explain myself. "It's the opposite. You and Oma and Dad—you're too special to me. I wanted to keep you to myself, separate from all the drama with friends and girls and stuff. But it didn't work."

"And now the Jasmine girl hates you."

"She called me an a—well, something I probably shouldn't say in front of my grandfather."

"Asshole?" His eyes sparkle.

"Yup, that's the one. Anyway, she's angry I won't let her meet you guys and that I'm closed off and don't tell her anything personal."

"I agree with the Jasmine girl."

"You think I'm an a-hole, too? Fantastic." I plop my cheek onto the table, staring at a bit of peeling vinyl centimeters from my face.

"No," he qualifies. "But I do think you're closed off with your family and friends. It hurts when you don't involve us in your life."

"I didn't mean—"

"Oh, I know," he interrupts. "And it's easy for me to forgive you. You're my oldest granddaughter, after all. And Jackson will come around if you talk to him. But what about Jasmine and your other friends? How can you get them to forgive you?"

"I feel like an apology isn't enough," I say, cheek still squished against the table.

"An apology is a start. But maybe action is also warranted. You need to prove you have changed, yes?"

If Dad's a quiet man, Opa is practically a monk. This has been the longest conversation we've ever had, and I'm touched that he cares this much about my high school drama. "Thanks, Opa. That's actually a pretty good idea."

He taps his head with a finger. "There's a reason I've been married fifty years."

"Do you think you could help me?"

He pushes my mug toward me. "First, tea. Then we can make a plan."

CHAPTER TWENTY-SIX

I SIT IN the half-lit shop, leg jiggling with nervousness. It's ten minutes before I told people to arrive, and I feel like I should be doing something. Oma and Opa and Dad are in the back, getting stuff ready, but Oma instructed me to wait out front to let the first people in. The shop's not usually open on Sundays, but she's making an exception for me. So I sit there, keys in hand, trying and failing to keep my leg still.

I hear a dainty knock on the glass door. The first arrival. I stand up, expecting to see Emilio or Madison or Garrett. I'd texted everyone from band whose numbers I knew and told them to spread the word: *My grandparents own Schultz Music, and they're letting you all get whatever you want for half off to get ready for state. Today, 4-6 PM only.* I'm still ignoring the single voicemail Jaz left the night before. No way I'm touching that.

But the knock isn't someone from band. Mom peers through the window, and when she sees me, she straightens and waves. "It's locked!" she calls, muffled by the glass.

I unlock the door and she bustles in, Jackson and

Caylee in tow. My brother doesn't meet my eyes.

"I thought you were resting at the hotel," I protest, though I know it's too late. This isn't how the plan is supposed to go. "We were going to meet you for dinner later."

"I got hungry early." She bulldozes through the aisles, knocking a box of reeds off a shelf with her giant purse. "Where's your father?"

"He's busy. Can you go up to the apartment to wait? We're kind of doing something right now."

She ignores me, looking around with a faint sneer on her face. "This place has always been so tiny. I've tried to convince your grandmother to move somewhere bigger, but she won't hear it. Not a very good business decision, if you ask me."

"Maybe they've got a good thing going," I say. "Not everything needs to be upgraded to a newer, flashier model."

I'm not talking about music shops anymore, and I can tell she knows it. She rolls her eyes at me and moves toward the back of the store. As she passes, I catch a whiff of wine on her breath. Thank god they've been taking Lyfts around.

"Mom." My frustration is plain in my voice. I do *not* have time for this. "Go upstairs."

"Miriam?" Dad emerges from the back of the shop, arms full of boxes. "What are you doing here?"

"Why does everyone keep asking that?" She throws out her arms, like the indignity of it all is too much to even fathom. "I'm *hangry*. I want to get dinner early. Sue me."

Of course, that's when Gavin and Madison show up. They look a little tentative as they walk in, though I can't tell if it's because of the scene I made last night or the scene my family's making right now.

"Hey, guys," I say through a fake smile. "Come on in! My brother can check you out at the register when you're ready."

Jackson shoots me a glare, but thankfully he heads toward the check-out desk, Caylee trailing after him. I owe him a good talk, but not yet. I have to deal with my parents first. I grab Mom and Dad by the wrists and yank them through the side door that leads to the apartment stairs, out of earshot of more arriving band members.

Mom starts in on me before I can launch into the speech I've started formulating in my head. "Who are all these people, anyway? I thought you were closed today."

To my surprise, Dad speaks up. "They're from Kendall's marching band. She wanted to help them out, so we're having a special sale day."

"So you're buying their friendship," she says to me. "Got to admit, didn't know you had it in you."

I remind myself that she's meaner when she's tipsy, but that doesn't stop my blood from boiling. I'm beginning to understand why "matricide" is a word.

"Miriam," Dad chides.

"What? I'm just saying. You and I both know Kendall doesn't really make friends. We used to worry about it all the time, back when you actually parented the kids. Remember?"

"Mom!" I shout. "You can't talk to him like that."

"It's okay, Kendall." Dad puts a hand on my arm and turns to speak just to me. "I can deal with her. I was the one who told her to come visit, after all. Wouldn't have done that if I couldn't handle it."

"You told her to come out here?" I look between my mother and father, stunned.

"I did," Dad says. "She brought up the idea of flying here during their fall break last week, and I actually agreed it would be a good idea. We could see Jackson and Caylee, and your mother and I would get a chance to talk some things out. Didn't think it would be *this* weekend, but I knew they'd be coming out soon."

Mom stands with her hands on her hips, watching the conversation but not butting in for once.

"Are you sure that was a good idea?" I'm still trying to wrap my head around everything. "What if you spiral?"

"Kiddo." Dad folds his arms. "I'm in a good place right now. My new doctor's got my meds at a perfect dosage, and the job has been helping me a ton. I haven't felt this stable in years, actually. You've been really busy with school and band, and I'm glad. You deserve to stop worrying about me all the time."

I feel like I've been riding the Sportster at full speed and suddenly hit a patch of gravel—not enough to crash, but enough to throw me off balance.

"You couldn't tell me they were coming?"

"I didn't think you'd take it well."

"Are you kidding me right now?" I run my hands down my face, shaking my head. "I don't even know what's going on. No wonder I can't get a relationship right. My parents are out of their minds." I set my shoulders, squaring off so I'm facing both Mom and Dad. "Okay, here goes. I've got some things to say.

"Dad. I'm mad you didn't tell me this weekend was your idea. I've been freaking out that you're gonna spiral this whole time, because I thought it was a surprise to you, too. Even if you don't want me to, I worry about you! Like, a lot. But I need to stop doing that. You're the parent, and I'm the kid. *Both* of us need a reminder of that."

I turn to Mom. "And you. I have a whole lot I could say to you. I'll start with this: I'm . . ." I struggle to find a good enough word. ". . . *Furious* with you for breaking our family apart. Maybe it was a long time coming, maybe it would've happened anyway, but there's absolutely no excuse for cheating. And your treatment of Dad afterwards was truly messed up. You were selfish, cruel, and on a personal level, you've ruined how *I* look at relationships now."

I pause to take a deep breath. I know I'm ranting, but I can't stop now. "Which sucks, because this year I met a girl I could've had something really, really amazing with. But guess what? Because of you, I have all these weird, twisted trust issues. No matter how hard I try, I can't seem to let myself be open with her. I screwed it up." My voice wobbles. "I screwed *everything* up at the exact time I started to fall in love with her."

Mom is stunned silent, and I have a brief moment of gratification as I take in her expression. Then my eyes focus in behind her, and I realize Jaz is standing in the doorway, mouth open, frozen on the spot.

"Jaz—" I start, but she's already in motion.

She ducks back into the shop, making a beeline for the front door. I ditch my parents in the hallway. *Not so fast, Whitaker.*

Carina watches Jaz pass and then gets in my way, arms folded. "What did you do this time?"

"I don't wanna hear it, Carina." I dodge her and speed-walk past, calling over my shoulder, "I'm going to *fix* things, all right?"

I'm determined not to stop, but then I see Adam quietly examining some cork grease on a display near the exit.

"I have a present for you," I say, walking sideways so I'm looking him in the eye but still moving. "I swear I bought it before all this. I'll even find the receipt if I have to prove it."

To my relief, he smiles. It's small, but it's there. "Okay."

"But first, I gotta chase down your sister. Stay here!"

By the time I make it outside, Jaz is already two blocks away, past the hardware store and the tea shop, sprinting down the sidewalk toward the bridge that crosses Whiskey River. I call her name, but she keeps going. I'm unsure whether it's because she can't hear me or doesn't want to.

There's no way I'm catching up to Jaz Whitaker, track star, on foot. I cut back through the building, ignoring the questions from my parents, and burst out the back to climb onto my motorcycle.

By the time I get out to the bridge, Jaz has made it across and turned onto the path that follows along the river's edge. I yank my handlebars to turn onto the street that runs parallel. When I hit a turn in the road, I pull over and park the bike. Jaz keeps running down the sidewalk. I roll my eyes and tear off after her.

She's not running as fast as she can. If she were, I would never catch her, I know that. But she doesn't make it easy, and I'm panting by the time I can snag her sleeve. I cling to that bit of fabric like it's a lifeline, and at my touch, she finally slows.

Jaz wheels around to face me. We stare at each other, catching our breaths.

"Why did you run away?" I pant. I am *not* cut out for this running thing.

She puts her hands on her hips, chest rising and falling. She swallows, brushes a curl out of her face, and finally says, "I heard what you said."

"All of it?"

"Just the end. You said you loved me."

"I said I was *starting* to fall *in love* with you. It's an important distinction."

"You're hot when you use words like 'distinction.'" Jaz cocks her head, already recovered from her unplanned sprint in jeans and flats. Her face grows more serious. "I ran away because I was about to come tell you I need time. And then you drop something like that."

"I want to fix things with you, Jaz," I say.

"Did you even listen to my voicemail?"

I look at my feet, sheepish. "I was too scared."

She rolls her eyes. "I said I wanted to meet up and talk. I threatened to break into the band office and steal your address if I had to. Fortunately Carina told me about this whole thing, so I didn't have to. Why didn't you just answer?"

"I was scared. I told you." I swipe a hand through my hair, but the wind is relentless, so I give up and let the hair blow across my face. "I realized that loving someone is complicated, and messy, and if it ends . . ." My voice catches. "If it ends, it's too hard. It hurts too bad." Jaz looks like she's about to speak, but I have to get this out. "But I've been thinking about it all day. About you, about my family, about living here. They're all worth the hurt. Even if there's an ending, or somebody leaves, or everything changes, the good stuff still happened. I want us, you and me, because we're *good*."

Jaz sniffs. She can't quite meet my eyes. "What if we mess it up?"

"We will!" At the twist of her mouth, I soldier on. "Because I'm not perfect, Jaz. No one is. And you're not either, though you're pretty dang close. You need to let people—especially yourself—be *human*." I stare out through the trees, at the river pushing over rocks and logs, always continuing on. "I wish you could see yourself the way I see you. You're this . . . magical being who appeared out of nowhere when I needed you most. When I moved here, I'd decided to recreate myself. I always felt too much, cared too much for the people around me. But my mom— when Dad needed her most, she left him out in the cold. And I was terrified of that happening to me. So I closed off, created another version of me. I called her 'New Kendall.'" I make air quotes, screwing up my face to show her how stupid I feel about admitting that.

Jaz nods along as if, suddenly, a lot makes sense. But she doesn't speak, not yet.

"I wanted to be this person I wasn't," I continue. "But you—you appeared out of nowhere. You picked me out and you wouldn't *let* me disappear into that version of myself, at least not all the way. You made me care. About Adam, Matty, even Carina. About the band, about your family. But Jaz, I care about you even more than I care about all that."

I reach out and take her hands. She's a little sweaty from the run, her palms warm and soft. She watches me with careful eyes, deep brown and fathomless, glistening on the surface as she lets me have my say.

"Jaz, despite my best efforts," I say, heart beating in my throat, "I think I've been falling for you since I saw you run past me on the street and I stared like an idiot. I fell a little more when I puked my brains out and you didn't blink. And then some more when you brought me that bug spray at band camp. It's been a whole long process. The hot tub definitely had something to do with it." I'm starting to ramble. *Rein it in.* "Anyway, the point is I want a relationship. With you. To be girlfriend and . . . girlfriend. Or whatever."

She's silent, inspecting me with parted lips. I squeeze her hands, feeling like I've just dumped my guts on the sidewalk. If she doesn't say anything soon, I'm going to completely bleed out.

Finally, she squeezes back. "Kendall." She pauses, starts again. "Kendall, I need time. I need to figure out what I want."

I'm already nodding, despite the pit that's opened in my stomach. I clear my throat, struggling to get my voice back. "Take all the time you need. I'll be here."

She releases one of my hands, raises it to touch my cheek. I close my eyes and lean into the feeling, wishing we could freeze in time right here, with a breeze carrying the scent of river and crisp oak leaves and something fried from the bakery up the street. I turn my face and kiss her palm, lingering there.

I open my eyes and look back at Jaz. The expression on her face is so warm, so affectionate, that I know she feels the same way about me. She hasn't said as much, but I meant what I told her.

I'll be here when she's ready.

CHAPTER TWENTY-SEVEN

"KENDALL, HURRY UP!" Dad calls from down the stairs.

I'm in my room, staring at the collection of equipment on my real, actual, non-futon bed. Dad and Oma assembled the IKEA frame for me last night, swearing in German the entire time. It's now topped with black socks, extra reeds, water, and a sack lunch. Dad brought my sax down with him, and I'm already wearing the black clothes I'll need underneath my uniform. But I can't help feeling like something's missing.

I glance at my nightstand. "That's it!" I proclaim, snatching the flip folder that contains all our pep band music.

It's section semifinals for the football team, which means that for the first time, the band will follow along and play pep band for them at an away game. We even get to do a shortened version of our halftime performance.

"Kendall!" There's a note of panic in Dad's voice, which must mean we are very close to being late.

Quickly, I swipe my arm around everything on the bed and throw it all into my backpack. I yank the zipper closed and careen out of my room. The apartment is spotless; Dad went on a cleaning spree the second the last box from the store reorganization was out. He beams at me as I meet him at the bottom of the stairs. Even though it's seven in the morning, he's freshly showered and shaven.

"Ready to win?" he says.

"You realize I have near-zero investment in the outcome of this game."

"That's the spirit," he says as I pass him for the back door. "Go Raptors!"

Dad's decked out in Itaska Marching Band gear. He purchased it the moment he signed up to be a volunteer earlier this week, though Miss Alvarez assured him band parents had no formal dress code. His therapist was thrilled with his decision, saying it would be a "great chance to get out of the house and bond with your daughter."

As Dad drives us to the school, my phone lights up with a text.

Mom 7:08 AM

Good luck at your competition 2day!!

Mom and I had a good, long talk after I returned home from chasing after Jaz. It was exasperating at times—she's *Mom,* after all—but we came to a sort of truce in the wake of my outburst. I guess I jarred her out of her usual self-centered haze for a minute. She even managed to apologize that I was the one to discover her affair, which was more resolution than I thought I would get.

Jackson wasn't ready to hash things out, but I got him to listen to my apology, at least. I hadn't realized how much my leaving hurt him. Caylee, too. I said sorry to both of them and tried to explain why I did it. I hope it was enough, but something tells me this will be an ongoing conversation. I'm still not entirely sure moving to Itaska was the right choice, but I also don't regret it. If I hadn't come, none of this would have happened. I never would have met Jaz or the rest of the band. I wouldn't have gotten to know Oma and Opa better. And things with my family might never have changed.

Before Mom, Jackson, and Caylee left for Colorado, we made plans for my visit over Thanksgiving break. I still have some mending to do with my siblings, and I hear there's a Turkey Trot at Garden of the Gods we can check out. I have this slightly unrealistic dream of becoming a good runner and impressing Jaz by the end of the semester. Maybe then she'll decide to date me.

So now Mom doesn't drunk text me, but she apparently does set an alarm for six in the morning, Colorado time, to incorrectly wish me good luck on a competition when it's only a football halftime performance. Truly out of her mind.

When we arrive at the school, most of the band is gathered on the lawn in the tentative light of sunrise. Everyone's cuddling for warmth, and I see some freshmen whacking each other with blankets. I say goodbye to Dad and climb out of the car, my eyes instantly zeroing in on Jaz. She's hugging herself and talking to Carina. The tip of her nose is dark red from the cold, and her breath comes out in puffs. I catch her eye and wave. She wiggles her fingers back and continues talking.

I don't go over. I've been giving her space since our talk, despite my pipe dreams of impressing her with my 5K prowess. I sit at Sarah's table at lunch. We've actually become pretty good friends after the whole homecoming debacle. Jaz said she needs time, and I'm determined to give her that.

I peer over Madison's shoulder to watch some video that she's showing Gavin and Matty. Alyssa's nearby under a tree, leaning on Emilio while Adam takes her wheelchair for a spin on the sidewalk. Garrett and Sam have their arms slung around each other, singing show music like a drinking song.

Alvarez calls for everyone to load up for the hour-long ride to the game. Dad has agreed to take the "terror bus" so I can still have some privacy, so I board alone and find a seat near the middle. Everyone else settles into their spots, filling the bus with excited noise.

I'm about to put my headphones in when I feel the seat depress next to me. I turn, and there's Jaz.

"Reese's Pieces?" She holds out a bag, already ripped open at the corner.

I'm struck breathless by her proximity. Her nose and cheeks are still a little red from the cold, and she watches me with a shy look on her face.

"Hey," I say.

"Hey." She grabs my hand and shakes some candy into my palm. Our legs are touching, our shoulders pressed together. I hold my breath, not daring to move as the bus pulls away from the school.

"Eat those."

Obediently, I toss a handful into my mouth. Jaz takes a deep breath.

"We're going to have to lay some boundaries," she says. "Figure out what a healthy relationship between us means. Something that works for *both* of us, not just one of us." Her eyes search my face, crinkled at the edges with the ghost of a smile. "I've missed you."

"I've missed you, too," I say through a mouthful of candy, worried if I don't respond immediately, she'll suddenly decide to change her mind.

"Also," she says, her shy smile growing into something more sure, "I love you."

It's like a bolt straight to my heart. She loves me. God, that feels good. Warmth spreads through my body, flooding every limb, and I'm dizzy with relief.

"I'm really, really glad," I say, leaning forward to touch my forehead to hers. "I love you, too."

We look into each other's eyes, a grinning, breathless staring contest. After a long moment, Jaz surges forward and presses our lips together. Oh, *this*. This is home and outer space and the deepest reaches of the Mariana Trench. Kissing Jaz is scary and also the most perfect, right thing in the world.

"All right, cool the PDA," Michael calls from a few seats up, but when we break apart, I can see that he's smiling. He shoots me a little thumbs up, then raises his arms to address the entire bus. "Who's ready to play at semifinals?"

I take an earbud out and offer it to Jaz. We listen to music while the sun rises out the window and the city races by. With my girlfriend's head on my shoulder, I don't think about the upcoming football game, or about what's happening tomorrow or in three months or after the year is over. I'm right here in this moment, and that's exactly where I need to be.

THE END

ACKNOWLEDGMENTS

Of all the books I've written, this was the scariest. I'm incredibly grateful to the people in my life who encouraged me to get Kendall and Jaz's story out into the world.

I owe an unpayable debt to my critique partners and beta readers, including Jo Doolan, Emily Steinbegle, Amryn Clark, Erin Mortensen, and the 2022 writing retreat crew.

Thank you to Marley Rose-Teter, whose editorial skills are precise and invaluable, and to Bailey McGinn, for her adorable cover design. To Ellen O'Clover, Jenna Miller, Christy Jane, and Zack Christensen, thank you for the parts you played in the release of this book.

I'm fortunate enough to have several networks of fellow writers that have sustained me during all the highs and lows of an author career. To the long-running YA Writers group chat, to my new community of Colorado YA authors, and to my RMFW and PPWC friends. Thank you for your critiques, commiseration, and confidence.

Special shout out to Arra Katona for being my first librarian advocate.

To Ben and my girls, all my gratitude for the patience and enthusiasm you continually grant me. I love you three more than anything in this world.

My greatest hope is for readers—young and old, gay and straight, musical and tone-deaf—to see themselves in my stories and know they deserve love without boundaries. If you have that in your life, I'm so glad. If you need to find them in the pages of a book, Itaska High will always be open to you.

ABOUT THE AUTHOR

Tasha Christensen believes the best love stories are found in the geekiest places. Her Itaska High series chronicles the romantic shenanigans of a high school marching band in Minnesota. When not composing tuba closet make-out scenes, she enjoys performing music, getting way too competitive about board games, and exploring the gorgeous Rocky Mountains. Tasha lives with her husband, daughters, and an overly affectionate dog named after her favorite Stranger Things character.

CONNECT ONLINE:
TashaChristensen.com
@author_tasha

OTHER ITASKA HIGH NOVELS:
As You Were

www.ingramcontent.com/pod-product-compliance
Lightning Source LLC
Chambersburg PA
CBHW061814190726

48289CB00007B/2197